STEPBROTHER VIRGIN

SUSAN STOKER

WRITING AS ANNIE GEORGE

ACKNOWLEDGMENTS

A, thank you for encouraging my crazy ideas and never telling me they're stupid. They *might* be stupid, but you're right there with me on my crazy train. Thank you.

My "Stalkers"- you guys support me in whatever crazy idea I have. You have no idea how much it means. You're the best!

1
MARRIAGE

Buck Thompson shook his head. People never ceased to amaze him...in some not so good ways.

"Pop, you can't be serious. How long have you known this woman?"

"Long enough, boy, and don't take that tone with me."

Buck sighed and ran his hand over his face in frustration. It seemed like his entire life he'd taken care of his dad. He'd always been more level headed and down to earth than his old man. Buck was only twenty two years old, but sometimes he felt forty two.

"Sorry, Pop. Go ahead."

"Loraine and I met about a month ago. She

brought her car in for some work, and it was love at first sight for us both. She didn't want to wait, and neither did I. We went down to the courthouse today and got married. I wanted you to be there, but I knew you had to work."

Buck bet he did. All he did was work. He worked at the golf course as a groundskeeper. He'd been working there since he'd graduated high school. The wages were all right, enough to keep both him and his dad fed, but Buck longed for more.

"Yeah, I had to work. What's she do for a living?"

"What do you mean?"

Buck repressed a sigh. "Work, Pop. Where does she work?"

"Oh, well that's the thing. She doesn't."

Buck felt nauseous. The last thing he needed was to have to figure out how he'd earn enough money to feed not only him and his dad, but Pop's new wife as well.

"She doesn't work?"

"Nope. She's got money. She don't need to work."

"Pop..."

"It's for real this time, son. I swear."

"That's what you said the last time."

"I know, but Kiki was lying when she told me she had an inheritance."

Buck barely kept himself from snorting. Inheritance his ass. He knew his dad had married her because she was young and had fake tits. "So this one's got money?"

"Yeah, *Loraine* has money. Apparently her first husband was killed while on the job because of faulty equipment and she got a huge settlement. Then her latest husband died leaving her a shit load of money."

"Uh huh." Buck barely listened as his dad continued to talk about his new wife and where she lived and how much money she had. Movement in his peripheral vision caught his eye. He looked over at four women in a golf cart driving crazily across the eighth hole.

"Hey, Pop, I gotta go."

"Did you hear me, son? We're going to her place to eat tonight and you need to be there."

"Yeah, okay. I'll see you at home later?"

"Sure thing. You'll see, you'll like Loraine. I'm sure of it."

"Okay, Pop. Later."

"Bye, son."

Buck clicked off his phone and shoved it in his back pocket. He immediately climbed into the golf cart sitting behind him and started after the women.

He'd worked damn hard that morning making sure the green was as perfect as he could make it. If the crazy chick driving that golf cart like she was a Nascar driver continued cutting across the pristine manicured course, there'd be hell to pay.

SUSIE HELD on for dear life as Maureen drove crazily across the golf course. She laughed as they hit a bump and all of them almost went flying out of their seats.

"Faster, Mo!" Loretta shouted.

"Yeah, go over there," Rachel pointed. "See what happens if you gun it over that hill."

Susie kept quiet and mentally shook her head. Mo was going to get them all killed, but she hadn't laughed this hard in a long time. She was twenty one and this was the first time in a long time she actually felt her age. Taking care of the entire household was stressful and as a result of dealing with all the people she had to manage with on a daily basis, she knew a career in human resources wasn't in her future.

Just before they reached the hill, and before Mo

could "gun it," another golf cart came flying from out of nowhere and cut them off. Mo shrieked, Loretta swore loudly, Rachel laughed crazily, and Susie squeezed her eyes shut and waited for the inevitable collision.

When nothing happened, except for them all almost being thrown out of their seats from the centrifugal force of Mo standing on the brake petal, Susie cautiously cracked her eyes open.

A man was standing in front of their cart with his hands crossed over his bare chest, seemingly unconcerned he'd almost been run over. Susie noticed that the chest his arms were crossed over was very muscular. He was scowling at them as if they'd just run over a puppy or something. Like usual, Mo didn't hold back her words.

"What the ever loving fuck was that?"

"What the fuck was what?" the man standing there retorted caustically.

Susie held her breath. Uh oh. He had no idea what he'd just done.

Mo stood up from the driver's seat of the little golf cart and went to stand in front of the man. "You almost killed us."

Not giving Mo a chance to continue, or indeed

start her tirade, the man broke in. "You see that?" he asked, pointing behind them.

Susie turned to look where he was pointing, and knew her friends were doing the same thing. She saw nothing but green as far as she could see. She turned back and eyed the man critically. He was probably about their age, it was hard to tell exactly. His T-shirt was tucked into the back of his pants and hanging down to the back of his knees. He had a smattering of chest hair, a scruffy, well groomed beard and a hint of a tattoo showing on his left hip. He had broad shoulders, the kind Susie had seen on swimmers in the Olympics. His jeans were well worn and the sneakers on his feet had definitely seen better days.

The golf cart behind him didn't have a backseat, instead it had a sort of truck bed, and was filled with all sorts of gardening materials. There were shovels, bags of dirt, a rake, and a bunch of other equipment Susie couldn't identify. It finally dawned on her that he most likely worked at the golf course and was obviously in charge of the gardening, or whatever it was called.

"See what?" Susie was shaken out of her perusal of the guy in front of them with Mo's acidic words.

"The fact that behind you are two long ass grooves in the grass where you stupidly drove your golf cart. You're supposed to stay on the concrete driveways. This is not the fucking beach or the mountains where you can just decide to go off-roading. Besides that, your friends were rattling around in that cart like they were kernels in a fucking popcorn maker and if you'd've hit that hill and gone over it, since none of you are wearing seatbelts, you all, most likely, would have been seriously hurt when you landed after you flew out of the cart." His words were one long run-on sentence, but his meaning was clear.

"Jesus, you might be a hottie, but you are one serious fuddy-duddy." That was Rachel, but she wasn't talking under her breath.

"Look, I spend a lot of time working to make sure this course is pristine and in top shape for people like your rich daddies to play golf on. As I said, if you want to go mudding, find a jeep and go up to the mountains. If you want to play in the sand, go to the beach and fuck off. But you do not drive a fucking golf cart like a bat out of hell through *my* golf course and fuck up the greens and the sod."

Susie just stared at the man. He was right, of

course he was, but he was being kind of a dick about it. And she certainly didn't like his comment about their daddies, why was it *guys* were always the rich ones? She spoke up. "Not everyone has a daddy, asshole. And my *mother* comes here to play golf. She's got money, you jerk, she can pay to have the stupid grass paved over more than once."

"It's sod, it's not paved," was his odd comment.

"Whatever," Susie waved her hand in the air dismissing his words. "My point is, loosen up. Seriously. Whatever stick is up your ass needs to come out. We're fine. You're fine. We were just letting off some steam. "

"Well, let it off somewhere other than my golf course."

Loretta chuckled. "*Your* golf course? I don't think it's yours. Hell, we could probably go back and talk to Mr. Dawson and get your ass fired anyway. How about it girls..." Loretta turned to her friends, "You saw him make a pass at me and grab my ass, right?"

Susie felt uncomfortable for the first time. It was one thing to get in an argument with the guy, it was another thing altogether to lie to get him fired.

"Yeah, catcalling and making obscene gestures isn't something Mr. Dawson would want his employees doing. Especially to young vulnerable girls like us...who have rich parents."

Susie could actually see the disdain that rolled off of the guy in front of them. If he was upset before, now he was absolutely *pissed*. His eyes swept over the four of them and then settled back on Loretta.

"Get your ass back in that cart and get the fuck out of here."

Loretta just rolled her eyes. "Figures, chicken shit. Come on, ladies. I think there are some mimosas calling our name back at the bar."

Susie climbed back into the back of the golf cart and grabbed ahold of the side. Mo gunned it and took off like a bat out of hell. The wheels turning left deep gauges in the earth. The last Susie saw of the man was him looking furiously at the back of the cart as they sped back the way they came away from him.

"What an asshole," Rachel said.

"Yeah, seriously. What the hell ever," Loretta agreed.

"We did fuck up the grass," Susie said tentatively.

"Who the hell cares," Mo bit out. "We just gave him something to do. It's not like it's that hard working here. He should've thanked us for saving him from boredom."

Susie kept her mouth shut. She had no idea what the guy did all day, but from the look of his dirty clothes and his sweaty chest, she didn't think he just sat around all day being bored. She didn't say anything though, knowing her friends would nit-pick the entire episode to death if the subject didn't get changed.

"Hey, I forgot to tell you guys," she exclaimed. "My mother got married!"

"What?"

"Holy shit!"

"No way!"

"Yeah, she met 'the love of her life,' her words, not mine, last month when she brought the Jag in because it was making that funny noise. The guy is about ten years older than her and is a mechanic."

"No Shit?"

Susie ignored Mo's comment and continued on. "Yeah, apparently he's like, completely broke, and will be moving into our house."

"Really? That's not a big deal, right? I mean, you always complain about how big the house is and how it's way too big for just you and your mother,"

Rachel questioned, holding on for dear life as Mo took a corner too fast.

"Yeah, but I didn't want her to marry again. You know how awful her other three husbands were. Shit, Larry made a pass at me at the dinner table one night and my mom was completely oblivious. I had to start hiding whenever I knew he was going to be around. It wasn't until she caught him in bed with Bambi, her yoga instructor, that she kicked him out and divorced him. Then there was Steve, yeah, you know what as asshole *he* was. Then she married Edgar..."

"Yeah, the eighty four year old gross old man." Loretta commiserated.

"Yup. She figured if the young guys weren't doing it for her, she'd go for an old one."

"Didn't she get like three gazillion dollars out of that one?" Mo asked as she pulled into a parking space for golf carts in front of the clubhouse.

"Yeah. He didn't have any kids and changed his will so she got most of it. You guys know she didn't need the money, but I can't say I'm sad Edgar's gone. That perverted old man pinched my ass every chance he could, and mother thought it was funny."

"So what's the draw of *this* guy?" Rachel asked, genuinely confused.

"I have no idea. I haven't ever met him. Mother just told me today that they got married. But she did tell me something else." She paused for dramatic effect.

"What?"

"That I'm no longer an only child. My new dad has a son. I'm a stepsister, and my new stepbrother is moving in along with his dad."

2

SURPRISE

"No way, no fucking way."

"Yes way, and stop fucking swearing at me."

Buck rolled his eyes at his dad and tried to reason with him. "There is no reason what-so-ever for me to move into some lady's house that I don't know just because you married her. I'm an adult, and now that you don't need me to fucking babysit you and give you money for the rent and food, I can stay here and you can go there."

Buck was pissed. He hadn't been home for thirty seconds when his dad had given him the "good" news that not only was he moving out, but Buck was going with him.

"You can't stay here."

"The hell I can't."

"No seriously, you can't. I already told the land-lord we were leaving. He's got it rented out to someone else already."

"What the all mighty *fuck,* Pop? When did you plan on telling me this? When you had your shit packed and you were walking out the door?"

"I did it for you, son. I know how hard you've worked, and it makes sense. We move in there, you save money, win-win."

"Jesus, Pop. First, I'm an adult, I don't need to follow your ass around like I'm an eight year old kid. Second, I've never even met this woman, and you want me to live in her house?"

"It's not like it's a two bedroom apartment, Buck. She lives in a fucking mansion. They have like ten people who live and work there full time. One of her ex-husbands left her a shit-ton of money, along with the money she got from her first husband's death. She's a billionaire."

Buck paced the small living room. His dad was sitting on the couch he'd picked up at goodwill for a steal. It only had two holes in it, but with the blanket thrown over the back of it, they weren't visi-ble. There were so many things wrong with what his dad just told him, Buck wasn't sure where to start.

"Pop. God. Okay, let's break this down. One of her ex-husbands?"

"Yeah, I think there's been like three or four."

"Pop."

"It's not a big deal, Buck. Hell, I've been married a few times myself."

Buck knew this. It was one reason he swore he'd never get married. It was too much hassle and he hadn't met a woman that made him want to risk tying himself to for the rest of his life...well, for as long as it might last at least. He'd dated one girl in high school, and when he'd found out she was only dating him because one of her friends' boyfriend told her he had a big dick and she wanted to see for herself, he broke it off. He dealt with enough drama at home with his dad to have any desire to deal with that shit in a relationship of his own.

He went back to questioning his dad. "*They* have people who work for them?"

"Yeah."

"Pop. They? Who the fuck is 'they'?"

"Oh, I thought I told you this morning...Lorraine has a daughter. She lives there with them."

"*Dammit*, Pop. So now you're a stepdad? How old is this daughter? Are you gonna be expected to go to fucking cheerleading competitions and ballet classes for Christ's sake? You couldn't manage to deal with me, how the fuck are you gonna deal with a kid?"

"Calm down. Jesus fucking Christ. She's your age, Buck. She's not a fucking kid."

Oh this just got better and better. "She's my age? And living at home? Why?"

"How the fuck do I know?" Buck could see his dad getting agitated, but didn't care. "I haven't even met her. Lorraine and I were getting to know each other without bringing our kids into it. You're both adults, so you don't have to approve of our relationship or our marriage."

"But you expect me to give up this apartment and come and live with you and this chick?"

"It's not that big of a deal. Jesus, Buck. I *told* you their house has a gazillion rooms in it. You won't even see them."

Buck just shook his head and stalked down the hall to his room, running his hand through his hair in frustration, leaving his hair sticking up in wonky angles. He couldn't afford to keep the apartment on his own salary. His dad was a fuckup, but he did contribute some money toward the rent. Buck had been saving to try to move out, and finally let his dad fend for himself once and for all, but didn't quite have enough to do it yet.

As much as he hated to admit it, his dad was right. He could save a lot of money living in this woman's house rent-free. And if Pop was right, and she did have as big of a house as he claimed, maybe it wouldn't be so bad after all.

"MOTHER, seriously, I don't understand why his son has to move in here. Isn't he too old to be living at home?"

"*You're* living at home."

Susie powered through the sting at her mother's words. She didn't *want* to be living at home, but her mother had no idea how to manage all the people she had working for her and the last thing she wanted was for them to not get paid, or to be treated like shit by her mom. There were times she loved her mother, but there were other times she had no idea how she was related at all.

"I am, but I'm helping you with the staff around here. It's not like I'm sitting around eating bon-bons."

"Susanne, dear...I want you to like your new stepbrother. I want you to get along. After all, you're family now."

Susie sighed and barely resisted rolling her eyes. She hated when her mom called her Susanne, and like hell was she ever going to call anyone her "brother." Her mom would most likely get sick of slumming it with this mechanic guy and divorce him, just as she had most of her other husbands. She thought of something suddenly. "Mother, please tell me you had him sign a pre-nup."

"Of course."

Susie sighed in relief. Her mother drove her crazy most of the time, but there was no way in hell she was gonna let all of her billion dollars fall into anyone else's hands. The guy would get a "good-will stipend," or whatever it was called, but he wouldn't be able to get his hands on most of her money. "Well, that's good then."

"Are you wearing that for dinner?"

"Yes, mother, I'm wearing this." *This* was a pair of jeans that fit her like a glove, high heeled boots, a black tank top that was cut low in front, and back. Susie wasn't going to change into a freaking prom dress just because she'd be meeting her mother's new husband and his kid for the first time.

"You look like a tramp."

"Mother..."

"You should change."

"I'm not changing."

"I'm not sure that's the impression you want to give your new stepfather and stepbrother."

"I don't give a shit, mother. And stop calling them that. We're both adults. We aren't going to start calling each other brother and sister."

Her mother opened her mouth to speak, but the doorbell pealed from far off at the front of the house. Susie watched as her mom stood up, ran a hand over her hair to make sure it was in place, and hurried out of the room. Susie snorted quietly, knowing if it was anyone else, her mom would just hang out in the sitting room until James escorted whoever was at the door to her.

Susie followed behind her mother slowly, dreading the evening. She couldn't believe two strangers would be moving into the house. Her mother had only known this Patrick guy for about a month...and he was a mechanic for God's sake. He was probably covered in grease and would most likely have no manners.

And Susie didn't even want to think about his son...her new stepbrother. What kind of weirdo would follow his dad and move into his new wife's house when he'd never met her? She supposed she'd find out soon enough. She could hear voices in the hall and reluctantly made her way to meet her new fucking family.

~

SUSIE WALKED into the foyer and saw James closing the front door. Her eyes went to her mother hugging a tall, surprisingly good looking, man who was obviously her mother's new husband.

He was a few inches taller than her mother, with brown hair. It was longer than it should've been, and he had a bit of a pot belly, but Susie was glad to see that he wasn't covered in grease and was wearing what she considered to be normal clothes. No overalls, just a pair of jeans, work boots, and a black polo shirt.

He put his hand around her mom's waist and turned to Susie. "You must be Susie. I'm Patrick. It's nice to meet you. Let me introduce my son." He turned and Susie noticed the guy standing behind him for the first time. She'd been so focused on seeing the man her mother had married that she'd momentarily forgotten his son would be there too.

"This is Buck, your new stepbrother."

Susie gaped at the man currently smirking at her.

She knew him. It was the groundskeeper from the golf course Mo had threatened that afternoon. Fuck.

He held out his hand to her and said, "Nice to meet you."

Susie automatically put her hand out to grasp his. When she did he leaned in and whispered for her ears only, "Surprise."

Double fuck.

3

___

MOVIN' IN

Dinner was extremely awkward, but Buck shrugged it off. He couldn't believe it when he'd walked in the biggest fucking house he'd ever seen and recognized one of the bitches he'd chewed out that afternoon at the golf course. Granted, Susie was the least bitchy out of all of them, but still. He took great pleasure in smirking at her and being over the top polite throughout dinner.

Pop's new wife didn't seem so bad, but then again, he just met her. Who knew what she was really like. There was a lot of superficial talk at the table, and Buck learned Loraine didn't work, and Susie didn't either. He'd barely resisted rolling his eyes at the pair of them. Didn't work. Jesus. He'd worked what seemed like every day of his life since he turned thirteen, and bent over backwards trying to earn enough cash to keep a roof over his and Pop's head and to eat.

After dinner they'd all gone into the sitting room to chat. Buck declined to sit and stood near the floor to ceiling windows, arms crossed across his chest, leaning against the wall, taking in the dynamics of his new stepsister.

When she wasn't around her bitchy friends she seemed very different. She wasn't shy, exactly, but she also didn't throw her weight around. At one point, when Loraine asked when Pop and he were moving in, that it wouldn't make a bit of difference to the "help," he swore he saw Susie flinch.

"I've told our landlord we'll be out by the end of the month," Patrick told Loraine.

"Good, that'll give the help time to get my step-son's room perfect."

"Yeah, okay," Susie said standing up abruptly, "I gotta go."

"Go? But sweetie, you need to get to know your new stepbrother."

"No, I gotta go do...something." Turning to Buck and Patrick she said through gritted teeth, "It was nice meeting you."

"I'll walk you out." Buck couldn't resist. He'd wanted to get her alone all night. He had some things he wanted to say to her.

"It's okay, I…"

"Great idea!" Loraine cut in. "You're siblings now, you should get to know each other."

Buck saw Susie did roll her eyes at that. He watched as she said good bye to his father and he trailed her out the door.

They walked to the end of a long hallway and Susie stopped and turned to him. She didn't beat around the bush. "Look, here's the deal. I didn't know you existed until today. I had no idea my mother got married until she sprung it on me earlier tonight. I don't want you or your father in this house."

"Wow, don't hold back," Buck said sarcastically, assuming his normal pose of arms crossed and leaning against the wall.

"I won't. I can't believe my mother got married again. She has no clue how to be a wife. I'm sorry to say this, but I don't think they're going to be married all that long. Don't get used to anything. You guys will be out sooner rather than later."

Buck couldn't really disagree with her, but her

words still pissed him off. They seemed like a dig against his dad. "Your mom better not hurt my Pop."

"Fuckin' A. Really? Your Pop..." she sneered the word, "was the one who married her after only a fucking month of dating. You know there's a pre-nup right? He's not going to get her billions."

"We don't want your money."

"Well, it sure looks like you could use it."

Buck felt every muscle tense at her snotty words. "Look, *Sis*, I don't like this any more than you do, but it looks like our parents have decided they're doing this."

"Fine, just stay out of my way and I'll stay out of yours."

"Fine."

"Fine."

Buck was ready to storm off to somewhere, anywhere other than standing in front of the pissed off, stuck up, bitch of a woman that was now his stepsister, his *rich* stepsister, when someone called Susie's name from down the hall.

"Jesus. Again?"

The soft words came from Susie. She was standing in the hallway looking at the three men standing there, obviously waiting for her. She looked back to Buck and said, "See you around," and she stalked down the hall toward the men.

Buck watched as the four had what was obviously a heated discussion. Susie's hands were flying a million miles an hour and the men were scowling at her. Buck shrugged and turned his back and headed back to the sitting room.

The men were obviously some of the hired help for the house and Susie was most likely trying to get the poor overworked employees to do something else that they probably wouldn't be paid for and would be taken advantage of.

How had this happened? He was relatively good looking, he was strong, he was a hard worker...how had he found himself being forcefully moved into a huge ass house, with a new stepmother and stepsister? It was crazy. As soon as he saved enough money he was out of there. Pop was officially on his own. He only had to stay away from his new stepsister until he saved that money. No problem. It was a big house.

SUSIE WATCHED Buck turn away and head back to the sitting room and she repressed a sigh. Thomas, Roman, and Tayzon had wanted to speak to her about her mother. It seemed she'd wanted to go shopping for a new outfit to wear to meet her stepson for the first time, and she'd "forgotten" her credit card. They might be rich, but Loraine was the cheapest woman Susie had ever met.

She did this all the time...forced their employees to pay for her stuff, under the guise that she'd pay them back later. Loraine had fired three people, accusing them of trying to cheat her by asking to be repaid for money they spent at the request of Loraine. Loraine would "forget" she asked them and accuse them of theft.

It wasn't until James steered them her way, and let her handle it that they'd been able to keep employees more than a couple of weeks.

"I'm sorry, Roman, I'll take care of it and get you paid back. Do you have the receipts?"

"Of course, I'm really sorry, Susie."

"Not your fault. You guys too?" Tayzon and Thomas nodded and handed her receipts from their outing as well.

Susie had thought about getting them a credit card they could use, but that seemed a bit too trusting, even for her.

"Find me tomorrow and I'll have the money to pay you back."

Each of the men thanked her again. When they turned to go, Susie put her hand on Roman's arm. "Hey, hang on a sec."

Roman nodded.

When the other men were gone, Susie said, "Mom got remarried today. Her new husband and his son will be moving in by the end of the month." She saw Roman flinch and powered on. "I know, it means more work for everyone. If you can talk to Alison and let her know. Mother will need some space made in her wing for Patrick, her new husband."

"Where do you want the son?"

"I don't care. As long as it isn't near me."

"No problem."

"I'll talk to Missy and let her know she's gonna have to increase the meals. I'll talk to mother and see if I can't figure out what these guys like to eat or what their schedules will be."

"Anything else?"

"That's all I can think of right now."

"Okay, I'll let the others know as well. Er...payday is still this Friday right?"

Susie sighed again and rubbed her temple. "Yeah. I'll have everyone's pay ready to go." She'd also taken over paying their employees because mother usually forgot that as well and then tried to stiff the employees claiming they were lazy or some such thing. Susie honestly didn't know why any of them stayed around. But at least it had gotten better since she'd taken over the managing of the house.

"See you tomorrow."

"Yeah, bye, Roman."

4

PAPER THIN WALLS

Buck lay on his bed and clenched his teeth. He'd been living with his new stepsister for a week now and he literally wanted to strangle her. For some asinine reason, his room was right next to hers. They were living in this huge house and they were practically on top of one another.

The only reason he didn't completely lose his shit was because Susie was obviously not happy about the arrangement either, so he knew she hadn't planned it. He'd listened in on a conversation she'd had with one of the employees where she lambasted him up and down and he'd apologized and said he thought she said to *put* the son next to her room rather than *not* next to her.

This might be a big fucking house, but that didn't mean it was constructed all that well. The walls were paper thin and he could hear every single thing Susie did in her room, and she could probably hear him as well.

Buck never bothered to sit down and eat with his Pop and Loraine, preferring to make his meals himself, something that Missy, the live-in cook scolded him about, but didn't seem to really mind. After dinner that night, he'd heard Susie on the phone with one of her friends, most likely one he'd met the day they'd careened around his pristine turf on their golf cart with. They'd been arguing about him. He'd only heard Susie's half of the conversation, but it'd gotten pretty steamy.

"No fucking way....yeah, but I'm related to him... yeah, I know, not really, but close enough....yeah, if I wasn't his stepsister...no you cannot! I don't want to hear you and him fucking in the room next to me... No! It doesn't make it better if you fuck at your house. Jesus, Mo!...He has his own bathroom so, no... You're perverted, you know that?...We still going out tomorrow?...That sucks...okay...later..."

It was quiet in her room for a while then Buck heard her TV turn on low. Then he heard it. Again. Fuck. He swore under his breath, knowing what she was doing. She'd done it every night since he moved in.

He could picture her, lying back on her bed, legs spread, vibrator on high between her legs. Her head would be thrown back, one hand at her tit and the other between her legs. Buck moved his hand to his own pants and quickly undid the buttons and shifted until he could get them down far enough to take his cock out.

He slowly stroked himself, not surprised how quickly he got hard. He could now hear her low moans over the voices on whatever show she was watching. His hand moved faster, squeezing the tip of his cock and massaging his balls with this other hand.

The sound of her vibrator now alternated between being muffled and then louder again, alerting Buck to the fact that she was now fucking herself with it.

Every damn night she tortured him this way. Hearing her moan was bad enough since he could only imagine what it might feel like inside her pussy, any pussy. Being a virgin at twenty two was hell, but he'd been too busy to want to make the effort it took to be able to get inside anyone's pants. But for the first time, he wanted sex. He wanted his stepsister. God help him.

SUSIE HATED when her friends constantly told her how hot her stepbrother was. She laughed off their comments, but living next to him was simply torture. She heard him getting ready in the morning, heard him getting settled at night. The walls were so fucking thin, and she'd had no idea they were before she'd gotten a neighbor.

She muffled her groan as she shoved the rabbit vibrator further into herself and adjusted the ears so they rested precisely against her clit. She then cranked the button at the end until it was buzzing on high.

Mo had wanted to know if she'd been able to catch Buck without any clothes on, but she'd been honest when she'd told her no. But she certainly wanted to.

Susie closed her eyes and imagined what the bulge behind Buck's pants looked like. He was stacked and he looked huge...she moaned then squeezed her lips together as she tried to keep quiet. She knew the walls were thin, that's why she turned on the television. She'd never masturbated so much before in her life. She couldn't go to sleep now without coming at least once.

She held the vibrator inside her and felt her orgasm move through her. She whimpered as her thighs shook and she curled up as it exploded though her body. She groaned one more time, long and low and then took a deep breath and laid back. She couldn't have been more surprised when she heard an answering groan through the wall.

Holy shit, was Buck masturbating too? She didn't hear anything other than that one groan, but that was all it took. Susie immediately snuck her hand down her belly and fingered herself frantically until she came again. Oh yeah. A wicked idea came to mind. Why should both of them suffer through taking care of themselves when they could take care of each other?

As she put her vibrator back in the drawer next to her bed and shut off the television, she worked through her plan in her mind. It might not work, but hell if she didn't want to try. Nothing gained, nothing lost...or however that stupid saying went.

She threw back the covers and pulled a T-shirt over her head. Not bothering with panties, if all went according to her plan, she wouldn't need any, she crossed her room and went out into the hall. Not taking the time to second guess what she was about to do, Susie walked the ten feet to Buck's door and opened it without bothering to knock.

BUCK LAY on his bed recovering from one of the most intense orgasms he'd had this week. He couldn't stop thinking about what Susie might look like as she pleasured herself and hearing her whimpers and moans pushed him over the edge. He was about to get up to clean himself off and try to get some sleep when he heard his door open.

His eyes shot to the door and he grabbed for the sheet he'd thrown off himself moments earlier. His stepsister stood in the door, her eyes devouring him as if she was about to eat her last meal.

"Hey, bro..." She said bro in a long draw our drawl. "Since we're both doing the same thing, want to do it together?" At the shocked look in his eyes, she laughed. "I've always wanted to be kinky...don't you want to screw your stepsister?"

5

VIRGIN

"Uh...."

Susie smirked at Buck. He was completely flustered and she continued to stand at his door watching him as he scrambled for the sheet and threw it over his lap. Susie wanted to pout. She'd looked forward to seeing his package, and what she'd seen from the door definitely was worth waiting for. He wasn't hard, but his dick had been lying on his lower stomach. Even not aroused, he was big. Susie licked her lips. How she wanted to get at that thing and see how big it could get.

"What the hell, Susie?" Buck complained belatedly. "I can't believe you just barged in here."

Noticing he hadn't ordered her out yet, Susie closed the door behind her and sauntered closer to the bed. Buck scooted away from her toward the other side.

"Look, I knew the walls were thin, but I didn't realize they were that thin until tonight when I heard you get off. I'm assuming the fact I've used my vibrator every night this week hasn't escaped your attention."

"Uh, no."

"Right. Then I feel it's my sisterly duty to tell you that while I've been fucking myself silly with that thing, I've been thinking about you."

"Fuck."

Susie was loving how uncomfortable Buck was. She had no idea he'd be this way. He oozed testosterone and was always bossy with her and she thought for sure he'd pounce on her the second she showed any interest. This was better. Way better. She grabbed the hem of her T-shirt and slowly drew it up her body until it was over her head. She dropped it on the ground and arched her back, thrusting her boobs out.

"So, you don't like my mom, I don't particularly like your dad, we're both pissed at them for being complete idiots, but that doesn't mean we have to forego what we both want just because they got married." Susie ran a hand from her hip up to her breast, then back down. She was a size fourteen and comfortable with her curves. Her breasts were large enough to take a man's cock between them, her thighs were curvy, her stomach soft, her hips large. The good thing about having some extra padding was that she could take a pounding with no problem, and she loved taking a pounding.

"I don't think..."

"Then don't think, Buck. I want you. I don't give a fuck that I'm your stepsister. We're too old for labels like that anyway. I want your cock. Please."

When Buck didn't say anything, but continued to lie on his bed looking befuddled, Susie took matters into her own hands. She leaned over and put her hands on the bed, trying not to spook him. She put one knee up, then the other one. She slowly crawled over to him, knowing her breasts were dangling down as she moved, enticing him. Buck couldn't take his eyes off her chest. She smiled. She had him.

Susie took hold of the sheet and slowly pulled it down until his cock was once more displayed. But lord, now she could see it up close and personal. As she watched, it slowly grew as blood once more filled it.

His tattoo was some sort of tribal thing. Susie had no idea what the fuck it was, but it didn't matter, it was sexy as hell. Seeing the remnants of his earlier orgasm on his stomach, Susie swiped one finger through the milky substance and brought her finger up to her mouth.

"Uh, I should clean up..."

"No fucking way. Stay there. This is sexy as hell." Susie, feeling bolder than she'd ever felt with a man before, straddled his thighs, keeping him in place. Buck's hands immediately went to her hips and gripped her...hard. His eyes were locked on her pussy, now spread open for his viewing pleasure.

"Like what you see?"

"Uh huh."

Buck didn't take his eyes off her and when Susie reached down and spread herself so he could take a more in-depth look, she watched as his cock grew even harder. She reached a hand down and grasped him. Her thumb and index finger didn't touch.

"Fuck, Buck. You're *huge*. Jesus. Can I taste?"

"Taste?"

Susie laughed. Buck could barely hold a conversation with her. His monosyllabic utterings were arousing as hell.

"Yeah, I want to wrap my lips around your monster cock and suck you dry." She watched as his eyes finally left her pussy and swept up to meet her own.

"As much as I don't want to admit this, I have to tell you..."

Susie ran her hand up his cock to the tip then back down, spreading his pre-come and previous orgasm around his length. "Yeah?"

"I haven't done this before."

Not stopping her hand's movement, Susie asked, "What? Gotten a blow job?"

"Yeah, and well, any of it."

"You're a virgin?" Susie asked surprised, sitting stock still. She watched as Buck's lips pressed together hard and a slight rosy hue swept up his face.

"Yeah."

Susie felt her heart start to beat faster. "Really? You're not shitting me?"

Buck simply shook his head and held himself stock still, as if waiting for her rejection.

"Oh my God, I'm not letting you out of this bed until you are thoroughly *debouched*. Incest has never looked so fucking good before."

Buck squirmed uncomfortably under her. "Can we not use that term please?"

"What, incest?"

"Yeah."

"But it is. Stepsister and stepbrother screwing each other's brains out. I'd make for an awesome book."

"This isn't a fucking book."

"No, it's not."

"Well, if you're gonna do it, get on with it. Otherwise get off so I can jack myself and get some sleep."

Susie smiled down at Buck, and moved her hand up and down his hard as nails dick again. "Oh, I'm gonna do it. I'm gonna make you come down my throat. Then I'm gonna teach you how to suck pussy, then you're gonna fuck my tits, then shove that monster so far inside me you'll feel it hit my cervix. Then you're gonna fuck me hard. And you know what, Buck?"

"What?" His voice was hard. His breaths were coming fast and furious through his nose and his hands were so tight on her hips, Susie hoped he was leaving bruises.

"Even if you come fast, cos' it's your first time, we'll keep practicing until you have better control. Don't worry."

"Condom?"

"I'm clean. Swear. I've never fucked without one."

"You on the pill or something?"

"Yeah, have been since I was eighteen."

Buck paused and Susie hurried, not wanting to let the chance to have sex with a virgin, without a condom, pass by. "Look, I swear to you I'm clean. I haven't had sex in like three months, I've always made the guy wear a condom. I don't want to with you. I know you're clean, if you haven't stuck this monster cock inside anyone else, then you're fucking clean. I want it. I want to show you how good it can be. Please?"

Buck nodded once, curtly. "Are we done talking?"

"Yeah, I think so."

"Then get busy, Sis. Suck my cock."

6

BUCK NAKED

Buck couldn't believe this was happening. Oh he'd dreamed it, but never in a million years thought he'd be lying on his bed, with his stepsister hovering over his dick staring at it like she couldn't get enough of it. He swore she was almost drooling.

He'd been embarrassed to admit he was a virgin, but hadn't expected it to actually turn Susie on more. He clenched his hands tighter around her hips as she started to slide backwards, finally he had to let her go so she could lay between his legs and get to his cock.

Buck knew this was not a good idea. Hell, sleeping with his stepsister could get him thrown in jail in some states, but he didn't give a fuck. He'd waited a long time to lose his virginity, and to lose it to the chick he'd been drooling over for the last week, and who he'd been listening get off each night? Yeah, he wasn't going to do anything to screw this up.

He inhaled as Susie gripped his balls in one hand and wrapped her other hand around the base of his dick. She tipped his cock up so it was standing straight up. She looked up at him as she licked the head once, twice, then a third time. He growled under his throat and put a hand on her head. "Quit fucking teasing, Susie. Do it."

"You're the virgin here, Buck."

"I might never have had this done before, Sis, but I know what I want. Suck it."

Buck drew in a quick breath as Susie did just that. Without losing eye contact, she wrapped her lips around his cock and slowly sank down on him. As she pulled up, her hand moved up too. Then she sank down again and her hand caressed down his length as she devoured him.

"Jesus..." Buck groaned.

Susie hummed as she continued to work his tool and he felt it in his toes.

"Yeah, Oh man. That feels so fucking good." Buck's cock twitched in her grasp as she moved the thumb of the hand that was holding his balls to caress the skin below. His hips jerked in her grasp and he felt Susie gag as his cock went a bit too far back in her mouth. Buck tried to relax, but it was nearly impossible. He felt come churning in his balls and knew he was gonna lose it way too quickly.

"Susie, back off. I can't....fuck...it's too fast."

She took her mouth off him long enough to murmur, "Give it to me, Buck. I want it," then she sank down on him again, jacking him off harder with her hand and she moved her head faster up and down.

Buck tried to hold on. He had no idea a blowjob would feel like this. He knew it would feel good, but not this good. He thought he was gaining control until Susie pushed down on him so far he could actually feel her swallow against the head of his cock. That, combined with her thumb caressing his back hole, pushed him over.

He grunted and grabbed her head with his hands as he spurted down her throat. Buck's hips jerked once, then twice, then a third time as he felt like she was draining him dry. He let his hands fall from her head, not wanting to choke her, and watched fascinated as Susie pulled her mouth off his dick and let some of his come fall out and onto the head. She looked up at him again as she licked his come off, cleaning his dick.

SUSAN STOKER & WRITING AS ANNIE GEORGE

"Fuck me."

It was all the warning he gave Susie as he leaned down and grabbed her under her arms. He manhandled her up and over to her back and brought his mouth crashing down on hers. Buck could taste himself, but didn't give a fuck. He'd once tasted himself after he'd jacked off, wondering what come tasted like. He didn't love the taste, but he didn't hate it either. But tasting it on Susie's tongue as they dueled back and forth was fucking fantastic.

Buck grabbed Susie's tits and squeezed as he continued the assault on her mouth. Finally he tore himself away and looked down. Her nipples were standing up and he loved how her flesh gave under his grip.

"Suck it."

Buck looked up and saw Susie grinning at him. "That's what you said to me, so I'm saying it back. Suck. It. Preferably hard."

Buck didn't hesitate. He leaned down and took a nipple into his mouth and sucked, hard. He felt Susie's back arch into him and her fingers grip his head tightly. But it wasn't until she moaned that he knew for sure he was doing it right. He used his teeth and pulled the erect bud in his mouth while at the same time squeezing and massaging both tits

46

with his hands. He lifted her right breast up and tried to see how much of it he could fit in his mouth.

When he heard Susie giggle, he lifted his head, not stopping his hands' movements. "What?"

"I don't think you're gonna be able to fit much of that in your mouth."

He smiled evilly, "I don't have to fit much in order to make these babies sit up and take notice."

"No shit." Was Susie's breathy response. "Are you sure you've never done this before? You're awfully good at it."

"I'm sure, but I'm thinking I'm gonna need practice. Lots of practice."

"Practice away, stepbrother."

"I will, if you'd keep your mouth shut, stepsister."

Buck heard her chuckle and he bent his head and got back to work. He sucked and nipped and squeezed her tits until she was squirming under him. He lifted his head and smiled at the light bruises forming on her skin. He liked seeing his marks on her. If this was the only time he'd get to have her, at least she wouldn't be able to forget it for a while.

"Down. Please go down on me."

Buck, enjoying having her at his mercy, decided to play. "Down? Down where? Here?" He circled her belly button, pushing his finger in while holding her firmly on the bed with his other hand on her breast bone.

"Noooooo, Fuck. Please, Buck."

"You know I've never done it, Susie. You're gonna have to talk me through it." Buck smiled again when she immediately agreed.

"Yeah, okay, I can do that. Down. Scoot down."

Buck didn't think he'd need all that much instruction, but he went along with her suggestion simply because it was where he wanted to be anyway. He pushed her legs apart and she immediately bent them up and held on to them with her hands. Her position opened her up for him and Buck got an up close and personal female anatomy lesson.

Susie was completely bare. He could see her pussy glistening with her arousal already. There were a lot of confusing folds, but Buck didn't hesitate. He separated her with one hand and pushed inside her with his finger. She was hot and wet. Fucking soaked.

"Oh God, yeah. Fuck me with your finger, Buck."

He did. He watched as his index finger disappeared into her folds, then as he brought it out he saw her juices covering it. It was if he'd just stuck his finger into a jar of dressing...he could see her come thickly covering his finger as he pulled it out. He pushed it inside her again, and pulled it out once more. Curious, he brought it up to his mouth and sucked it into his mouth. It wasn't anything like he'd ever tasted before. Not sure he liked it, Buck brought it back to Susie's pussy and pushed inside her again. This time before he pulled it out, he felt around. Her inner walls were spongy and hot.

"Oh yeah," Susie moaned. "Do that again."

Buck hadn't realized that she'd be able to tell what he was doing. He did it again, but couldn't get very good leverage. So he pushed his middle finger in with his index finger. Yeah, now he could use both to caress her from the inside out. When Susie jerked in his hold and grunted, he figured it felt good to her too.

Instinctively knowing it would tease her, he pulled his fingers out, but kept holding her open with his other hand and put them both into his mouth. Yeah, her taste was growing on him. If asked, there would be no way he could describe it to anyone, it was completely unique, but it was exciting as hell. He, Buck Thompson, was finally gonna get some tonight.

"Suck me, Buck. Use your mouth."

Buck eased himself up on his knees between her legs and lifted Susie's ass up until it rested on his knees. He put his hands under her butt and leaned over. He licked once from the bottom to the top, like she'd done to him, like a lollipop. Susie groaned.

"Again, but this time lick my clit at the top when you get there."

Buck did as she asked, finding the hard nubbin with his tongue when he reached it. Fascinated, he brought one hand up and spread her folds apart and saw the little bundle of nerves. It was small and pink, and Buck swore as he stared at it, he could see it throbbing. He blew lightly and smiled when Susie jerked in his hold.

"Like that?"

"Oh god, yeah. Please, suck my clit."

"But I want to taste you...right from the source."

"Yeah, okay, but I'm telling you, you could lick down there all night long and I wouldn't come. You have to concentrate on my clit."

"Patience, Sis," Buck teased.

"I thought I was instructing you here."

"You are, but I want to play too. I've never seen a pussy up close and personal. I'm educating myself."

"Fuck."

Buck ignored the exasperation in Susie's voice

and leaned over her again. He held her lips apart and licked up and down her entrance. Her unique taste again covered his tongue. Buck continued lapping at her, watching as she squirmed in his hold and as she clenched every time he had pity on her and licked over her clit.

Juggling his hold on her, Buck took one hand and laid it across her hip bones and held her hood open so he could have direct access to her clit. He brought his head down and started lapping lazily over her clit. At the same time he pushed two fingers back inside her.

"Oh yeah, *yeah*, Buck. Fuck me with your fingers as you suck on my clit."

Buck did as she asked. He closed his mouth over her little clit and sucked on it as he did her nipple earlier. She jerked violently in his arms and it was all he could do to keep her from jerking out of his hold. He pushed down harder on her hip bone with his forearm and moved his fingers in and out of her faster.

"Oh god, Yeah, right there. Harder. Lick me harder, Buck. I'm gonna...yeah...keep going....Uhhhhhhh."

Buck could literally feel Susie come apart in his arms. Her pussy squeezed his fingers tightly and he forced them to keep moving in and out. She bowed upward and curled into him as her stomach contracted and he watched in fascination as every muscle in her pussy clenched in ecstasy.

When she flopped back on the bed, Buck ordered, "Hold your legs again."

"What?"

Buck pushed her legs upward until they were lying against her chest. "Hold. Them."

Susie did as he asked and he scooted down until he was lying down, with his head at her pussy. "I gotta taste you this way. I want to know what your come tastes like right after you explode."

Then he bent his head and devoured her. He nipped and licked and sucked. Her juices were soon soaking his face, but Buck didn't care. He wanted it all. She tasted fucking delicious and he'd made her this way. He couldn't believe he didn't like her taste at first. As far as he was concerned, he was now obsessed. He wanted to lick her come out of her every time she orgasmed from now on.

"Buck, Jesus, stop. I'm sensitive."

Buck grabbed Susie's hands when they pushed on his head. "I'm not done. I want you to come again. Come on my face, Susie. Let me have it. You're delicious."

"Oh lord. I've never..."

Buck felt ten feet tall. He might be a virgin, but he was doing something to her she'd never had before. Fuck yeah.

He covered her entire pussy with his mouth and licked and sucked what he could reach. His nose was buried in her stomach and it was hard for him to breathe, but he didn't care. Buck shoved his hands under her ass and lifted so he could get at her more easily. Sensing she was tiring of holding her legs, he stopped messing around and attacked her clit again. He took it between his teeth and lashed it with his tongue. He couldn't believe his fucking tongue muscle was actually getting tired, but he wasn't going to stop until she came all over him again.

Finally she semi-screamed and bucked up against him once more. He brought his finger up and harshly massaged her clit so she'd continue to come, but he moved his head down so he could drink her release down again.

Finally feeling her quivering with exhaustion, he moved up. Susie dropped her legs, lying panting on his bed. Buck smiled down at her. He put both hands on the mattress next to her shoulders and kneeled over her. His cock brushed against her belly and left a smear of pre-come on her skin. He reached down and took himself into his hand, balancing on one hand.

"I'm going to fuck you now," he informed her seriously.

He watched as Susie opened her eyes and looked up at him. She brought both arms up and over her head. "You're good at this for a newbie."

"Thank you."

"You know where that goes?" she teased.

"Yeah, I'm a guy. I've watched porn. I know where it goes."

"Fuck me, Buck. Fuck your stepsister."

Her words shouldn't have turned him on, but they did. What they were doing was so taboo and off limits, but he didn't give a shit. Apparently, neither did Susie.

Buck rubbed his cock up and down her slit, feeling their fluids mix. He shoved the head of his dick against her clit and felt her jerk under him.

"Stop fucking around. Do it."

Buck lined his cock up with her pussy and didn't fuck around. He pushed inside a woman for the first time, pushed inside Susie, hard and fast.

"Oh my God, wait, shit, oh man."

Buck didn't wait, but slowed his push a fraction. He shoved himself in until he could feel his balls up against her ass. He dropped to his elbows and stayed extremely still. He waited until Susie opened her eyes and looked at him.

"Holy shit," she breathed. "You're huge."

Buck chuckled and they both groaned at the feel of him laughing. "I can't believe how good this feels."

Now it was Susie's turn to laugh. "I take it this meets with your approval?"

"Fuck yeah it does."

"You need to move."

"No."

"No?"

"No, if I move, I'm gonna come, and I want to memorize everything about this first time. I want to remember the feel of your inner muscles clenching on my cock as I pushed in. I want to remember the way you quivered under me as I hit bottom. I want to remember the feel of your juices soaking my balls. I want to remember watching your tits twitch as I pushed inside. Most of all, I want to remember you calling out my name as you orgasm, and that won't happen if I move right this moment. I'll come and leave you hanging."

"You just made me come twice, Buck. Your turn."

"Nope. I find it makes me feel ten feet tall to make you come. I'm not sure what will happen after tonight, but if I have my way, I'll have the chance to do this again and again, but mark my words. Every time we fuck, you're gonna come. You're gonna come more than once. And if you haven't come at least four times for my one, then I've failed."

"Buck..."

"So, tell me how to make that happen, Susie. What do you need to come two more times? I want to feel your muscles squeeze my dick while I'm inside you more than I want to get off myself right now."

"My clit. I can't come without my clit being rubbed."

"Then you're gonna have to do it. I can't hold myself up and rub you at the same time. Besides, I wanna watch you do it. I need to see what feels good. All those times you masturbated in your room I imagined watching you finger yourself. Show me. Do it."

Susie didn't hesitate. Buck watched as she snaked her hand between them and slowly started rubbing herself. Buck backed his hips up just a bit, and even that small amount of friction almost threw him over the edge. He gritted his teeth and watched fascinated as Susie frantically rubbed her clit. She was a lot harsher than he thought she'd be able to take, and he took note of it.

"Move, Buck. Please? This feels good, but I want to feel you take me hard."

"Don't stop rubbing yourself. If you do, I'll stop."

"I won't. Jesus, please. Fuck me, Buck. Fuck like it's your first time," she smirked up at him. "I can take it. I can take you. Fucking fuck me already."

Buck did as she asked. He pulled back to the tip and slammed back inside her. Susie grunted and shifted on the bed, but recovered and kept rubbing her clit. "Yeah, again. Fuck me."

He did. He pulled back again and again and pounded into her. After four strokes Buck knew he wasn't going to last. He pushed himself all the way into her and leaned up. He pushed Susie's finger away from herself and used his thumb to harshly rub her clit. She thrashed under him and he used his index finger to pinch her clit...hard. "Fucking come. Now."

She did and Buck gloried in it. He felt every twitch of her pussy against his dick. She squeezed him so hard it almost hurt. Almost. He shoved himself inside her as far as he could, loving the feel of her bathing his cock with her juices. Looking down at Susie, Buck clenched his teeth and lost the iron control he'd been holding onto. Without pulling out even a millimeter, he shot inside her. He could feel his dick twitching and jumping inside her cunt, and it felt fucking awesome.

Buck kept himself shoved inside Susie and lay down, pulling her over him as he went. He put one hand on her ass and kept her from moving backwards.

"I gotta go clean up."

"No."

"No?"

"No."

"Buck, I know you don't know this, this being your first time and all, but it's what women do."

"No."

"Buck."

"Look. I just fucked for the first time. It was fucking awesome. So much more than I could've imagined, then I *have* imagined. I want to stay inside you. You're warm. You're wet, and the way you squeeze my cock every time you laugh or move feels like nothing I've ever felt before. It's late. We're gonna lie here buck naked and sleep. Me inside you. You loving it."

"Buck naked?"

"Yeah."

Susie giggled and repeated, "Buck naked?"

Buck smiled, realizing what he'd said. "Yeah, Buck is naked and so is Susie. Now hush."

Buck lay in bed long after Susie fell asleep, amazed at what had just happened. He still wasn't sure he liked Susie all that much, and had no idea how she felt about him, but he knew he liked the sex. He could deal with the rest. Now that he'd had it, he wanted it. Every fucking day if he could get it. Susie had no idea what she'd done.

7

A+

Susie woke slowly, feeling completely rested for the first time in a long time. Thoughts of dealing with the crap from her mom's employees and even of her mom's new husband, far from her mind. She shifted, or tried to shift, but realized she was immobile on her back. She opened her eyes and looked down, feeling hands holding her hips.

Buck was lying between her legs, much as he had last night, and he was staring intently between her legs. Susie felt him run a finger between the lips of her sex.

"What are you doing?" She asked groggily, knowing the question would sound stupid at any time other than first thing in the morning before she was completely awake.

"I'm watching my come drip out of your pussy."

Susie blushed and put her hand over her eyes. She'd been completely shocked when Buck had told her he was a virgin last night, but he'd certainly burst that cherry with flying colors. "Uh, Buck, that's kinda gross."

"Like fuck it is."

"Guys just don't do that."

"They don't?"

"No."

"Why not?"

"Huh? I don't know. They just don't."

"What do they do?"

"They tell us to get up and go wash up. Or we just do that, get up and wash up in the bathroom away from them. I honestly haven't had a guy come inside me, so I'm not sure how well 'washing up' would do in that case, but either way, that's usually what happens."

"Well, fuck that. This is fascinating."

"Buuuuck."

"It *is*. I get that you've probably never seen this before, but you should. You're wet, of course, but differently than when you came. You've got my come dripping out of a small slit at the bottom of your pussy. It's not gushing or anything, but it's dripping down on your ass then down to the sheet.

I guess this is what they mean by the 'wet spot' huh?"

"Oh my God, seriously. You are insane."

"We slept connected most of the night. I swear to God my cock was semi-hard all night. Tucked in nice and tight in your wet warm pussy, it never felt so good."

Susie could feel herself blushing, but Buck didn't stop.

"I accidentally rolled over this morning and lost you, but I felt a rush of wetness on my dick as I pulled out. I had to look. My dick acted like a plug, and when I slid out, so did our juices."

Susie watched as Buck took a finger and pushed it slowly and gently inside her. She arched her back and felt her nipples grow taut. It actually felt really good. She'd never had morning sex, but she could see she'd been missing out.

Buck took his finger out and brought it up to his mouth and sucked. "We taste good." He put his finger back inside and pulled it out again. This time he bought it up to her mouth. "Taste us."

Susie automatically opened her mouth and Buck eased his finger inside. Their flavors exploded on her tongue. Musky, tart, and definitely unique.

"Good, yeah?"

Susie could only nod as Buck dipped his head. "Oh God, Buck."

"Shhhhh, I'm hungry."

Susie held on to the sheets for dear life as Buck once again devoured her pussy. After he'd made her come twice, he rolled them until she was straddling his lap. "I have a lot to make up for. Ride me. While we fuck, tell me all the other positions I have to try."

"I've created a monster," Susie said, obeying him by lifting up, tucking his cock against her hole and sinking down. She propped herself up on his chest.

"I know there's missionary, I think we covered that adequately last night...what else?"

Susie could hardly concentrate. Sitting on Buck this way made him feel like he was going so much deeper than when they were in the missionary position.

"Well, there's doggy style."

"Self-explanatory, go on."

Susie grunted as Buck grabbed hold of her tits and squeezed as she bounced up and down on him.

"On our sides, reverse cowgirl..."

"What's that?"

"Well, what we're doing now, but with me facing the other way."

"Hummmm, but then I can't do this..." Buck took both nipples between his fingers and squeezed hard.

"Oh my God, Buck."

"Keep going. What else?"

"Against the wall, on a table, me bent over a table, both of us sitting up, spooning, you in a chair....Buck!"

Buck had moved one hand and was flicking her clit as she rode him. Then he moved his hand so it was around the base of his dick and he could feel her take him on every down stroke. It was the most erotic thing she'd ever experienced.

"Have you done it all those ways?" He asked unexpectedly.

"What?"

"Have you fucked in all those positions?" Buck repeated impatiently.

"Uh, No. Only doggy style and reverse cowgirl."

"Good. We'll learn them together. Now, fuck me, Sis. Show me how it's done."

Susie slammed herself down on Buck and moved her hips in a circle, she lifted then did it again. She grunted, moaned, and generally used Buck's cock to get herself off. After she came she looked down sheepishly. For a moment she'd forgotten who was under her.

"God, that was fucking hot. My turn."

Susie shrieked as Buck turned to the side and dumped her off of him. He immediately turned her onto her stomach and got behind her. "No time like the present to knock one more off the list." He pulled her hips up and before she could really even prepare, he'd thrust himself inside her.

"Oh yeah, Fuck that feels good, Buck."

"I feel like I'm a lot deeper this way," he said as he pumped in and out of her.

"Yeah, I think you might be."

"And I can see this right here in front of me." He widened his stance, thus widening Susie's legs in the process. She was splayed out in front of him. Buck put his thumb against her back hole and rubbed.

"Have you done this?"

Susie tried not to tense up. "I tried it once with a boyfriend, but it hurt and we stopped."

"I bet I can make it not hurt....no...don't clench, I'm not doing anything right now. Don't worry. I'm just playing a bit. Nothing to worry about."

Susie tried to relax, but it was hard. She felt Buck pull out all the way and she whimpered. He stuck two fingers inside and wiggled them around before pulling out again and placing his cock back at her entrance and pushing back in. He then took his two soaked fingers and used them to lubricate her ass.

"Buck..."

"Shhhh, I said, don't worry. I won't do anything you won't like. I liked it when you rubbed me here while you were taking my cock down your throat, I bet you'll like it too."

And she did. Buck rubbed and massaged and when he brought the other hand down and rubbed her clit at the same time he thrust in and out of her, Susie couldn't even remember her own name.

"Yeah, fuck you are sexy, Sis. I've got my thumb buried in your ass up to the knuckle and you're shoving back against me so hard I know you love it."

And she did. It didn't hurt, but made everything seem so much...more.

Buck pulled his thumb out but continued to rub her clit roughly with his other hand. He held her hip tightly and growled. "Come now, I want to feel you squeeze my dick before I come again."

Susie exploded and dropped to her forearms, not able to hold herself up. She felt Buck remove his finger from her clit and hold both her hips in his hands as he slammed inside her. He stiffened up and Susie knew he was about to come.

She was surprised when he abruptly pulled

out and grunted as he came all over her lower back and ass. He'd been so obsessed with watching his come slide out of her that she figured he'd take every opportunity to continue to do so.

"Oh yeah, Susie. I never understood the allure of coming on a woman. I've seen it in pictures and in porn films, but didn't get it. I fucking get it now."

Susie felt Buck running his hands over her back, spreading his come into her skin.

"Lay down on your stomach. That's it."

He helped her ease down and Susie put her hands under her cheek. She lay under Buck as he straddled her thighs and used both hands to caress and massage his release into her back and ass. She felt his semi-hard cock resting against her ass cheeks. She moaned when she felt him harden against her again.

"Have pity on me, Buck. No more. I'm already sore."

"If I could, I'd keep you here all fucking day, but I've got to get to work, and if I'm not mistaken, the help is probably losing their shit over one thing or another."

"Mmmmmm."

"I see how you take care of them all, Susie. Don't

think I don't. Just lay here for a bit. Relax. They can get along without you for an hour or so."

"Mmmmm-kay."

"Stay here in my bed, covered in my come. I want to remember this moment all day while I'm cutting grass and spreading mulch."

"That's not very romantic."

"I'm not romantic, Sis, but I can tell you one thing. You're sleeping here tonight. And the next night, and the next. I'm not nearly done fucking you. I have a lot to learn and you have a lot to teach me about all this fucking business. I gotta get up to speed."

Susie smiled and turned her head to look at Buck. "I think you got an A on the assignment last night."

"Good. Now sleep for a bit longer. I'll head your mother and Pop off and give you some time."

"Thanks."

"You're welcome."

Buck got up, running his hand through his come on her back one more time. Then he ran his hand through her hair, grinning when she grimaced up at him.

"Gross."

"Nah, it's hot as fuck. If I thought you'd do it, I'd ask for you to not shower this morning."

"No way in hell."

"Didn't think so. Kiss me then, and I'll see you tonight."

Susie leaned up a fraction and Buck moved the rest of the way. He took her mouth as if he'd been giving morning-after-kisses his entire life. When they broke apart, Susie's head dropped back down on his bed. She felt him run his fingertips down her back, over her ass, over her thighs and calves and to the tip of her toes before she lost his touch.

She dozed lightly as Buck showered, got dressed, and left the room. Knowing she had to get out of bed, Susie kept her eyes closed for as long as she could. Jesus, she'd come into Buck's room last night hoping to be able to have a quick fuck. She had no idea she'd introduce her stepbrother to the joys of sex, and that he'd excel in it so much. If she could grade him, he'd definitely get an A+.

8

THE PLAN

A month had passed since Buck had started fucking his stepsister. Most of the time he could ignore the fact they were essentially related. When his cock was buried deep in her pussy, he didn't think about anything but how good it felt. He'd gone from being a virgin to a porn star and all it took was one night, one night with Susie. He wanted her all the time. Buck had no idea what was normal when it came to sex, but having one, maybe two orgasms every night probably wasn't. He didn't give a shit.

He and Susie had done everything and anything. He always made sure she came first, and second and third, before he took his own pleasure. They hadn't ever used a condom, and even when Susie had her period, he didn't give her a break, not that she wanted one. They experimented with shower and tub sex, and simply put a towel down on the bed before they'd gotten down to business.

Everything wasn't all sunshine and roses, however. Their relationship was good, even if they both put the small matter of them technically being related to the side. Their parents' relationship was not good. Pop was a hard man to live with, and Loraine was used to doing what she wanted, when she wanted. Pop hadn't quit his job, even though it wasn't as if the small amount of money he didn't drink away was helpful to the household in any way, but he was quickly finding out that Loraine was much more demanding now that they were married than she'd been during the month they'd been dating.

He'd talked to Susie one night while they lay exhausted in bed after a long fuck session that involved him tying her hands behind her and bending her over the mattress. She'd told him how she desperately wanted out of the house, and could actually leave at any time since she came into her trust fund the year before. She apparently was a billionaire in her own right, which surprised the shit out of Buck. She didn't act like any billionaire he'd ever met...not that he'd ever met any others.

But she didn't feel like she could leave because her mother had no clue how to manage her house or the employees. Susie had gone away to college for one year and when she came home for the summer there was only one employee left and the house was a disaster. Her mother didn't really even seem to care. Susie explained to him that she thought her mom was mentally unstable and how she felt stuck.

Buck told Susie about how *he* was stuck with his dad because Patrick couldn't manage to save enough money to feed himself or pay the bills because he'd drink his salary away.

"How the hell did two dysfunctional people manage to find each other?" Susie had bemoaned. "We're never getting out of this house."

"We are. There's no way I'm living with Pop for the rest of my life. I'm twenty two years old, it's time for me to be on my own," Buck told Susie, pulling her closer into his arms.

"What are we gonna do?"

Buck ran his hand over Susie's hair, down her back to her ass and pulled her closer into him. He was still semi-hard inside her and he hitched her leg higher up and over his hip.

"Does it bother you that we're related?" he asked her seriously.

"No." Her answer was immediate and heartfelt, and made Buck sigh in relief. "You?"

"Fuck no. And it's not like we're really related. We didn't grow up together, I don't like you like a sister, and the way things are going, we probably won't be related for too much longer."

Susie murmured her agreement and buried her nose in the crook of his neck. "So again, what are we gonna do? If they break up, we'll be right back where we were before."

"I have an idea."

"What?" Susie propped herself up on an elbow, making him harden as he felt her clench against him with her movements.

"We feel guilty because we feel like we need to take care of our parents, right?"

"Yeah."

"You have enough money to hire someone to do it."

"I've tried that."

"No, I mean a professional. I think if you make it clear up front they are there to manage the staff and generally keep your mother under control, it'll go better. Don't beat around the bush. Tell them straight up what the issues are and what you expect from them. Also, get someone with an

73

advanced degree in Human Resources or something. They should be used to dealing with employees. You can pay someone enough to make it worth their while. Even if they don't live in the house, they can work here every day and keep things running."

"Hmm."

Susie's mumble, wasn't totally encouraging, but Buck powered on. "You can still stop in and check up on things. It's not like you're gonna move across the country and never talk to your mother again. You can keep your finger on the pulse of what's going on here, and have a place of your own."

"What about you and your dad?"

"That's tougher. I don't have the money to hire someone like you do."

"Yes, you do."

"No, I don't."

"Yeah, Buck. You do. Well, your dad will. He signed a pre-nup, but mother always includes a 'bonus' in the pre-nups she makes her fiancé's sign."

"What are you talking about?"

"Buck, if your dad divorces my mother, he gets a million dollars. Nothing more, but he'll get that."

Buck turned abruptly until Susie was under him. Because he was still hard inside her, he was able to do it without his cock falling out of her pussy. "Are you shitting me?"

"No."

"Does my dad know?"

"I have no idea."

"If he got hold of that money it'd be gone within a year. He'd drink it all fucking away."

"But you could hire someone to manage it for him, couldn't you? If you invested it, then had the manager pay things like rent and his other bills, and even hire someone to buy food, you'd be off the hook. You could do like me, check on him during the week and stuff."

"Holy fucking shit, Sis. This could work." Buck smiled down at Susie. "We need to go apartment shopping."

"Rachel has already told me I can live with her."

Buck tilted his head and narrowed his eyes as he looked down at Susie. "What would you say to moving in with me?"

Susie inhaled sharply, but didn't say anything.

"Think about it. We've basically been living together for the last month. After work we eat, then come in here, or go to your room and fuck, then sleep together all night. We eat breakfast together when we can, we hang out on the weekends. Hell,

I've even suffered through a night out with you and your bitchy friends." Buck smiled as he said the last and sighed in relief when she smiled back up at him.

"You *did* suffer that night didn't you? They wouldn't keep their hands off you."

"Fuck yeah, the more Loretta drank, the more she kept trying to grab my dick to see how big it was."

"But their faces when I told her your dick was off limits and all mine was priceless."

Buck got serious again. "Susie, I want you in my bed every night. I love fucking you, I think you love me fucking you. We have a good thing here, why mess with it?"

"Do you love me?"

The question wasn't entirely unexpected. "Not yet." Buck knew his words might hurt her, but he wanted to be honest. "We haven't been together long enough for me to know if I love you."

"Thank God. I was afraid you were gonna have some virginal attachment to me that you thought was love."

Buck chuckled, loving how realistic Susie was. "But that doesn't mean I want to go out and stuff my dick in anyone else's pussy or that I'll allow you to open your legs for any asshole who wants in there."

Susie smacked his shoulder. "Like I was gonna let anyone else in here. Hell, Buck, you keep me on my back every chance you get. It's not like I have any time to even look for anyone else."

"Fuck yeah." Buck thrust his hips into Susie and she groaned. "This is my fucking pussy. You popped my cherry and you have to teach me all there is to sex, I know you're not done yet."

"God, you feel so good. I have no idea how you can stay hard so long."

"It's you. All I have to do is think about your pussy and how it tastes and how it feels around my cock and all the blood drains right to the tip."

"I'm assuming we're about to fuck again here, but before we get too carried away, are there any legal or moral reasons why we shouldn't do this?"

"No."

"Buck..."

"Tell me you're moving in with me."

"I'm not sure..."

"You're moving in with me." Buck pulled out until just the tip of his cock was inside her. He wasn't above using sexual blackmail to get what he wanted. And what he wanted was Susie's pussy whenever he wanted. And that meant she had to live with him.

Susie grabbed his ass trying to bring him back inside. "Buck, in me. Now."

"You're moving in with me."

"Okay, fine. Whatever. Fuck me, Buck. Seriously."

Buck slammed his hips down and ground against Susie, rewarding her for her words. He spent the next long while rewarding his stepsister for her correct answer.

When they once again were laying, satiated for the moment, wrapped in each other's arms amidst the strewn around blankets, Buck said, "Tomorrow we'll start this plan in motion. I know my Pop and he's not going to put up with your mother's shit much longer."

"Okay, Buck."

"I don't give a fuck where we live, so you're in charge of finding us a place."

"Yeah."

"I'll talk to Mr. Dawson at work and see if he can't give me the name of a good money manager for my dad, and for your mother if you want it."

"That's a good idea."

"You okay with looking into an HR type person for around here?"

"Yeah. I'll ask Missy. She might be the cook, but I

know she's worked for several different households. I'll see if she has any good ideas. I trust her."

Buck put both hands around Susie's head and tilted it. He leaned over and nipped her earlobe before whispering, "I didn't want to move in here. I thought you were a stuck up bitch, but I'm fucking glad it worked out. My cock is glad. My former virgin status is glad. And I've never had a sexier, fuckable, stepsister before."

Susie giggled and Buck could feel the goose-bumps that broke over her skin. "I never dreamed my stepbrother could be so insatiable and would have such a big dick."

"You love it."

"I do love it."

"Shut up, Sis. Otherwise I'll have to fuck you again."

"Is that even possible?"

"Keep talking and find out."

"Goodnight, Bro."

"Goodnight, Susie."

9

IT'S DONE

"You asshole!"

"You bitch!"

"I can't believe you just called me a bitch!"

"You started it by calling me an asshole!"

Susie sighed as she stood outside the door to the sitting room listening to her mother and Patrick fight. They literally sounded like they were in junior high school, instead of the adults they were. It certainly hadn't taken long for her mother's new marriage to fail. Susie had no idea what they were fighting about now, but whatever it was, was probably something stupid.

Luckily she and Buck had put their plan into motion the day after they'd talked about it. She'd had a long talk with Missy and was relieved the wonderful cook was one hundred percent behind it.

"Girl, we all know you're only here to take care of us, and we appreciate that more than you know. But you're young, you should be out living it up in the real world, not dealing with the issues your mother creates."

Susie had agreed and given Missy a big hug after they'd talked. She had some great suggestions and Susie had found a woman and had lined her up to manage the house, and her mother, once she finally did leave.

She'd also gone house hunting with her friends. It was fun, even listening to the incest jokes Mo, Loretta, and Rachel kept lobbing her way. In the end, she'd found a kick ass townhouse that was perfect. There was a balcony off the master bedroom that overlooked a man-made lake. The entire top floor was the master suite, complete with a separate shower with three shower heads, two sinks, a separate little "room" for the toilet, and a Jacuzzi tub. The downstairs had a half bath, a beautiful kitchen with granite countertops and stainless steel appliances, a little dining room off the kitchen, and a huge open living room.

It was horribly expensive, but Susie didn't care. Buck wasn't thrilled with the price, knowing he couldn't afford it, but Susie took him down her throat and held him on the edge of orgasm until he finally agreed. Of course he'd turned the tables on her and refused to let her orgasm afterwards...at least until he'd gotten his fill of drinking her juices, but in Susie's eyes it was a win-win.

The security at the place was top notch. She and Buck had talked further about their situation and neither wanted his dad or her mother popping in unannounced, so the gates surrounding the property were a welcome addition.

Not knowing exactly when they'd be moving in, Susie decided to err on the side of caution and with a cash payment, settlement happened very quickly. Now they were slowly bringing stuff over to the house, so when Loraine and Patrick finally pulled the plug on the marriage, they'd be ready.

"I'm done with this shit."

"Good, 'cos I'm done with it too."

"How come I didn't know what a bitch you were when we were dating?"

"Maybe because you were too interested in getting in my pants than getting to know me?"

"So, you admit you're a bitch."

Ouch. Susie suppressed a chuckle. It wasn't nice, but it was an awesome comeback by Patrick.

"I want you out...today. And take your smelly, hanger-on of a son with you."

"Oh, I'll get out, but not until I'm good and ready."

"Fuck that. You'll get out today."

"I don't have any place to go." Patrick's voice was now a little whiny.

"I don't care."

Susie thought this would be a good time to make her presence known. She and Buck were supposed to do this together, but he was working and she since this was happening now, she had to deal with it. She pushed the door open and walked into the lion's den. Both occupants turned their heads to stare at her.

"Hey."

"Susie, now is not the time," her mother told her acidly.

"No, I don't suppose it is, but here I am anyway," Susie said breezily, feeling unaccountably happy that this moment was finally here and she'd be getting out from under the oppressed feeling she'd always had living with her mother.

"Excuse me?"

"Sorry, Mother, but it's obvious you and Patrick

83

haven't been getting along recently. I'm sorry about that." She tried to sound contrite, but it didn't quite come out that way.

"I don't know what business it is of yours," Patrick grumbled.

"Well, technically it's not. And as your daughter, and stepdaughter, it really shouldn't be any business of mine. But since you two argue all the time, and don't care if Buck or me are around to hear it, you've made it our business."

"I don't think I like your tone."

"Well, here's the thing, mother...I don't like the way you've been treating Patrick. I know he's not the perfect man, but it's not fair. You didn't give him a fair chance."

"Yeah."

Susie turned to Patrick at his comment. "And you haven't really given my mother a fair shot either. She's got money, and is used to a certain way of life. You should've tried to understand that more."

"What's your point?" Patrick growled.

"My point is that you guys need to be done with this marriage. It's obviously not working, which Buck or I could've told you from the start. Patrick, you need to get out of here and start living your own life again. Mother, you need to lighten up and see if you can go one fucking year without marrying anyone. You need to get out and do something. Volunteer, something. It's not healthy to hang out here and shop. You need more."

"Listen here, bitch."

"That's enough, Pop." Buck's voice was low and angry. He'd obviously walked in and heard his father's words. He put his hand on Susie's shoulder and continued. "Everything Susie just said is dead on accurate. Don't take your frustration about your situation out on her."

Susie watched as Patrick finally clued in to what had been under his nose the entire time he'd lived in the house.

"Are you seriously banging your stepsister?"

Buck didn't even hesitate. "Yes."

"Susie!" Her mother's tone was shocked.

"Yes, it's true."

"But he's your stepbrother."

"Mother, seriously? It's not like we grew up together or anything." She turned to Patrick. "You moved your son into this house with you. We're the same age. He's hot. What did you expect?"

Neither had anything to say. Buck brought the

conversation back around to the issue at hand. "Right, okay, you guys are done. That's obvious. Pop, I got you an apartment last week. You can move your shit in today."

"Good, we can get out of this looney bin."

"I'm not coming with you."

"Huh?"

"I'm not coming with you," Buck repeated patiently.

"But..."

Buck knew what his dad was concerned about. "Right, I'm done spending my hard earned money on food because you've spent your entire paycheck on booze. You'll be responsible for your own rent and your own food. But since I know that's probably beyond you, since you haven't learned how by now, I'm afraid there's no hope, I've hired someone to manage the money you'll get from this divorce so you can't spend it on inappropriate shit."

"He's not getting any of my money."

It was Susie's turn to address her mother. "Yeah, he is. Remember the pre-nup, Mother? He's getting a million bucks. He can't touch the rest of it, but you both signed fair and square."

Loraine crossed her arms across her chest and

pouted, then said. "Fine. They can get out and we can go back to the way things were."

"Nope, I'm moving out as well."

"But, I need you."

"No you don't. You need someone, yes, but it's not going to be me. I'm sick of mediating disputes from the help because of something you've done. I'm tired of paying them back money you spent because you 'forgot' your credit cards. You have to grow up, Mother, and I'm done. I've hired you a manager to keep your employees happy, because lord knows you don't care, and to manage your money. You have plenty of it, and you need to learn how to spend it appropriately."

"You can't do that."

"It's already been done."

Before Susie knew what was happening her mother walked up to her and smacked her across the face. Susie stepped back on a foot and would have fallen if Buck hadn't been standing there. Susie put a hand up to her face in shock and pain. Her mother had never struck her before. What the hell?

Buck moved swiftly, pulling Susie to his side and then pushing her behind him, so he blocked any access her mother might have had to her.

"And that's one of the reasons why we're all leaving. You act like a child, don't take any responsibility for yourself , your employees or anyone else around you. You can't see that you've been treating your own daughter like a slave. She hasn't moved out before now because she's been worried about you, and you don't give a fuck. No one puts their hands on her in anger. Not even you. Now, I suggest you get your shit together and figure out what you're doing to do, because Susie and I are out of here tonight. Your new house manager will be here in the morning to introduce herself to you and your staff. I suggest you play nice with her because otherwise you'll find yourself trying to run this house by yourself, which is something I know you can't do."

Susie peeked around Buck and saw her mother looked pale. Her lips were smooshed together and she was breathing hard. She hated to see it, but she felt as if a hundred pound weight had been removed from her chest. Susie put a hand on Buck's back and rubbed, showing her appreciation for him standing up to her. She sidestepped and addressed her mother.

"Mother, I appreciate all you've done for me, but it's time I lived on my own. I want to finish college. I want to get out into the world."

"I've given you everything."

"You have," Susie agreed immediately, "But it's time you let me go. We're both adults. You're a billionaire, but you might as well not have any money. You don't know how to manage your money or spend it. You act like spending twenty bucks to give your driver a tip is a crime. You need to live a little, mother."

"I can't believe you're choosing your stepbrother over your mother."

Susie rolled her eyes at her mother's continued emphasis on her and Buck's supposed familial relationship. She didn't take her eyes away from her mother's, but felt Buck's arm go around her waist as he pulled her into his side in silent support.

"I'm not choosing Buck over you, Mother. I'll still be in town, and I have every intention of coming to see you all the time. I love you, and I don't want this to end our relationship. But I'm twenty one, I need to get out, live my own life."

"With him?" Her words were dripping with disdain.

"Yeah, at least for now." Susie couldn't help but poke the bear a little. "And you know what? If we get married, you'll be related to Patrick again."

Buck chuckled under his breath and said, "Low

blow" as they watched both Patrick and Loraine blanch.

Buck was apparently done with the conversation. "Okay, family meeting is over. It's done. Pop, I'll help you move your shit to your new apartment. Susie and I will move our stuff out over the next couple of days. Loraine, contact your lawyer and get the divorce paperwork started. That's it. It's over and done."

Susie looked up at Buck and swallowed hard. They'd had the conversation recently about love, and she'd been relieved that Buck hadn't fallen in love with her, but now? Looking up at him as he held her against his side, protected her from her mother's wrath and made it clear where he stood about anyone hurting her? Yeah, she could feel herself leaning more toward wanting him in her life forever.

"Come on, Susie, we've got shit to do."

Susie nodded and put her arm around Buck's waist as he led them out of the sitting room.

"We've got to get some ice for your cheek."

"I'm all right."

"I can't believe she hit you."

"She didn't hit me, she only smacked me."

"Same fucking thing."

"Not really."

"I'm not in the mood for you to argue with me, Sis."

Susie smiled as he led them to the kitchen. Missy quickly got an ice pack put together and tsked over the short version of the story Buck told her. Missy said she'd make sure the other employees knew the new house manager would be there the next day and that they'd know what was up with everything.

Buck thanked her and herded Susie out of the kitchen and up to his room.

"Where are we going now?"

"I have to spend the rest of the day moving Pop's shit out of here and into his new apartment. I have to listen to him bitch about your mother and calm his shit down about what he's gonna live off of. He'll probably give me shit about you and me, and that pisses me off. I don't give a fuck what anyone else thinks about us, but it's gonna piss me off to hear it just the same. While I'm doing that, I have to leave you in this fucking house with your mother who is most likely still pissed at you and who just hit you. I'm stressed out and pissed and worried as fuck."

Susie stumbled alongside Buck, knowing she wouldn't fall because his arm was tight around her waist, and tried to soothe him with a light touch to his stomach as they hurried down the hall. "I'm sorry about all that, Buck, but where are we going?"

"My room. I need to erase the memory of all that shit by eating you, then fucking you. Maybe if I put your taste in my mouth instead of the pissed off taste I've got in my throat, I can function for the rest of the day."

Susie smiled broadly. She was all for that.

10

EXPERIMENTATION

Susie sat on the couch in the townhouse and blindly watched the television. She was a bit nervous, as Buck said he wanted to try something different when he got home. Susie had no idea what that something different could be, as she thought they'd done just about everything they could do already. They'd worked their way through the list she'd made that first night, and then some. They'd already christened every room and every piece of furniture in their house. They'd even tried anal sex. It wasn't something Susie wanted to do every night, but Buck had taken his time and gone as slow as she needed, and she'd found some enjoyment out of it.

The last three months had had their ups and downs. Her mother hadn't completely forgiven her, but she hadn't barred her from the house either.

Susie still went over there every week to make sure all was well. She might be irritated with her mother, but she didn't want her to end up on the streets or be taken advantage of by the employees either. The new house manager was working out very well. Everyone seemed to like her and even her mother grudgingly admitted she was doing a good job.

Buck's pop was settling into his new routine as well. Since neither Loraine nor Patrick contested the divorce, it was settled quickly and the million dollars was transferred into an account Buck had set up in his dad's name. Patrick didn't have direct access to it, he had to go through the account manager, and Buck. He complained bitterly at first, but since he had a good place to live, food on the table, and he could use all of his own salary for booze, he'd settled down fairly quickly.

Buck continued to work at the golf course, but Mr. Dawson had been proud of the way he'd stepped up to take care of his father and had taken him under his wing. If things went the way Mr. Dawson suggested, Buck would quickly be moving up the ranks at the club.

Susie bit her thumb and jiggled her leg. She'd gotten some information from the local community college about finishing up her degree and moving on to get her Bachelor's. She wasn't sure exactly what she wanted to do, except that she preferred to work with numbers instead of people. She'd had enough of that to last a lifetime.

The conversation she and Buck had all those months ago had been weighing on her mind more and more. Somehow she'd fallen completely head over heels in love with her stepbrother. Well, technically they weren't stepbrother and stepsister anymore, but they still called each other "Sis" and "Bro" all the time.

But Susie wanted more. She had no idea what Buck thought of her. Since he'd been a virgin when they'd met, she didn't want him to suddenly get the itch to try out other women. They still had sex almost every night, but just the thought of Buck giving his cock to any other woman made her insanely jealous. It was *her* dick, dammit. Hers.

The sound of a key in the lock surprised Susie and she turned stood up and faced the door as Buck walked in. He was sweaty and had dirt stains on his clothes, but it only made her hotter for him.

"Hey. How was your day?"

"Good. Yours? See your mother today?"

"Yeah. All seems well there. You hungry?"

"No. Stopped on my way home. You?"

"Not really."

They looked at each other across the room for a moment before Buck turned and locked the door. He turned back to her. "I have to shower. While I'm cleaning up, I want you on our bed, naked, hands over your head. I'll be in as soon as I'm done."

"I'm nervous." The words came out of her mouth without thought.

Buck smiled and laughed a short laugh. "I'm not going to say you shouldn't be, if that's what you're hoping, but I'm thinking you're going to love everything I do to you tonight."

"Oh Jesus."

"Go on. Head upstairs. I'll be up in a sec."

"Ok, Bro."

BUCK FOLLOWED Susie up the stairs. He was hard just thinking about what he had in store for her. He wasn't one to watch porn, but he'd seen a video online that had stuck with him. He'd wanted to try it for ages, and tonight was finally the night. He'd ordered what he needed and knew they were in a solid place in their relationship. He couldn't wait to try it out.

Buck wanted to take their relationship to *that*

next level, but wasn't sure how. He was in love with his former stepsister and wanted her, and everyone else, to know it. He wanted to publically claim her and make her promise that her pussy was his and his alone. He wasn't ready to propose marriage, wasn't sure when he would be. But he didn't worry too much about that as he knew Susie felt the same way about marriage as he did. They didn't have very good role models in that area, and it'd be a fuck of a big step if they did ever get there.

But he needed her to acknowledge what was between them was more than fucking. More than just being roommates, more than being fucking stepsiblings. It might have started out that way, but it wasn't anymore.

Buck smiled at the sound of Susie opening and closing drawers in the bedroom as he stepped into the shower. The three shower heads felt amazing on his skin, but he didn't dawdle. He had a plan and needed to see it through.

He stopped out of the shower and rapidly wiped his body down with a towel, taking off most of the moisture from his skin. He brushed his teeth quickly and dabbed on a bit of cologne. He knew how much Susie loved the smell of it on his skin.

He strode into the bedroom and felt his cock

jump at the sight of Susie on their bed. She'd done just as he asked. She was completely naked and had her hands resting above her head on the pillow.

Instead of heading toward her on the bed, Buck entered their walk-in closet and got a bag he'd hidden behind some of his clothes in the back corner. He brought it back into the room and put it down on the floor next to the bed.

He leaned over and caressed Susie's arms, from her palms, down to her shoulders, then back up. "Relax, Sis, this is gonna be fun."

"For you or me?"

Buck smirked, she knew him so well. "For both of us."

"What's in the bag?"

"You'll find out soon enough. Lift up, I need to move the comforter out of the way."

Susie did as he asked and lifted her ass just enough so Buck could push the sheet and blankets out of his way to the foot of the bed.

"God, you smell delicious." Buck leaned down and nudged her legs open. When Susie's legs opened enough so he could see her glistening pussy, Buck rewarded her with a long lick between her folds. "And you taste even more delicious."

Susie moaned and shifted under him.

"Keep your arms above your head." Buck didn't wait to see if she did as he asked, knowing she would, and he leaned down and brought out one of the items in the bag. It was a pair of leather wrist cuffs and a long piece of rope.

"Holy shit, Buck."

They'd played around with restraints before, but this was the first time they would use actual wrist cuffs. There was a wide band of leather that buckled shut. The inside was lined with fur so as not to hurt the wearer and there were two large silver rings on the outside. Buck leaned over and grasped Susie's right wrist and buckled the cuff on. He then did the same to her other wrist.

"How do they feel?"

"Good."

"They don't hurt? I didn't make them too tight?"

Susie shook her head and looked up at him with wide eyes.

"Okay, next step then." Buck took his time tying the ropes to the slats in the headboard. He made sure they were just the right length and that they were tied securely. When he was sure they were just how he wanted them, he turned his attention back to Susie.

"Wrist." His dick jumped when she didn't say

anything, but simply held her right wrist to him for him to attach to the rope. He did the same with the other wrist.

"Now, how does that feel?"

Buck watched as Susie tested her bonds. Her arms were bent at the elbow so she had some room to move, but he knew the minute she realized how vulnerable she was when her eyes dilated and she looked up at him uncertainly.

"You are fucking gorgeous, Sis. I swear I'm not going to do anything you won't like. No blood, no knives, no torture. Just pleasure. Yours, then mine. Okay?"

"Okay, I'm just not sure why this feels so different than before."

"Because it is."

Susie smiled at him. "That didn't make any sense."

Buck leaned down and kissed her, but didn't elaborate. "You ready for more?"

"More?"

"Yeah. More."

"I guess."

Buck leaned down and pulled out the next item from his bag. It was another set of cuffs, this time for her ankles.

"Uh, Buck, we don't have a footboard to attach anything to."

"Why don't you let me worry about that?"

"Shit, okay. Yeah."

Buck went through the same process of buckling on the ankle cuffs, making sure they were snug, but not too tight, before pulling out a long bar with hooks on each end.

"Oh fuck me. Is that what I think it is?"

"Yup, a spreader bar. I'm going to attach your ankles to it and you won't be able to close your legs to me."

"I don't think that's necessary, Buck."

"Well, if we don't need it, great, but I'm going to truss you up anyway, just in case. I'll give you a choice though."

"Nice of you," Susie said sarcastically, but with a smile on her face.

"Knees up, or legs lying flat?"

Buck watched as Susie thought through her options. He could almost see her thinking.

"Legs flat."

He chuckled, knowing for what he had in mind, legs flat would actually be harder for her, and easier for him. "You got it." He got to work buckling her ankle cuffs to the pole. Once he was done he turned a screw and slowly expanded the bar, spreading her legs further and further apart.

"Hey!" Susie complained lifting her neck to look down at his handiwork.

"Easy, Sis," Buck soothed, putting a hand on her stomach. "You're good." He separated her legs until they were as spread as he could make them and still have her be comfortable. He retightened the screw on the pole until it was tight again. "Test it."

Susie rolled her feet, but the pole didn't move. She lifted her knees, but could only lift them around six inches before she dropped them back to the mattress. "Uh, this is...awkward."

"No, it's beautiful. I have access to every part of you and you can't stop me."

"Buck..."

"Again, stop doubting me, Sis. I'm not going to hurt you." Buck spent some time reassuring Susie, running his hands up and down her legs, massaging and caressing her. He leaned over and kissed her stomach, then the undersides of her breasts, then her neck, and finally he gave her his mouth. As they kissed, Buck used his hands to massage her tits and to pinch and pull on her nipples. Finally he pulled his mouth away as one of his hands snaked down to her pussy.

"I love this pussy. You're always so wet for me. You can take me as hard as I wanna give it to you. It tastes fucking fantastic. I can't get over it."

"Buck..."

"I have no idea what other pussy tastes like, but I know you've ruined me for life. Seriously, Susie. I don't even give a shit about any other woman but you. I want this pussy for myself. For always."

"Oh my God, Buck."

"Shhh, before you say anything, I want to see what I can make this pussy do."

"What do you mean?"

"You always come so beautiful for me. You get so fucking wet my cock thinks it's entered heaven every time it gets inside you. But I don't think you've gotten as wet as I think you can get."

"Huh? Buck, seriously, you make me come at least twice before you'll put your dick in. That's as wet as it gets."

Buck didn't respond, but leaned over to the mysterious bag on the floor one more time. He fiddled with something near the floor and then finally sat up. He was holding a Hitachi massager.

"Oh Jesus fuck."

The massager was electric and he'd plugged it in while he'd been near the floor. The device had two settings, low and high, and had a large round rubber head on it. It was designed to massage out kinks in people's backs, but every women knew that wasn't the best use for it.

"I saw a video online once. Ever heard of forced orgasms, Susie?"

"Buck, no."

"Your mouth says no, but your tits say yes." Her nipples had grown tight at his words and Buck could see her squirming on the bed. "I want to see how this works. I've seen women actually squirt come out of their pussy while their man uses this on them."

"I don't think those videos are real."

"Oh, they're real all right. Come on, what do you have to lose?"

"I'm not sure about this."

"I know. And you weren't sure about anal sex either. Or that time we had sex on the balcony. Or when you came to see me at work and I fucked you against the door of the storage shed...and all those times worked out all right in the end, yeah?"

"Yeah, but..."

"Okay then. Now hush. I want to see what this pussy's capable of. Let the poor virgin play, Sis."

"Poor virgin, my ass."

Buck ignored her and moved so he was sitting

between her legs. They were spread apart far enough that he could actually sit between them, his legs thrown over her hips with his feet up by her head. He shifted around until he was comfortable, well as comfortable as he could be with his cock harder than he thought it'd ever been.

"Ready?"

"No."

"Good. I'll start slow." Buck turned the massager on low and ran it up and down her belly, watching as Susie breathed heavily in and out. He moved the wand so the head was massaging the undersides of her breasts, then he put it directly on her nipple.

"God..."

"Feel good?"

"Oh yeah. Fuck yeah."

Susie was squirming under him now and pulling slightly on her arms. Buck put the heel of his free hand against her pussy and caressed her roughly, trying to warm her up for the feel of the massaging head. She was wet, covering his hand with her juices. He moved the massager to her other nipple and barely kept himself from drooling at the way they stood straight up.

"Here we go, Sis." Buck ignored her moan and moved the massager down her belly to her clit. He touched it once and watched as Susie jumped under him. "Easy."

"Fuck easy," she grumbled, but smiled as she said it.

Buck placed the vibrating head directly on her clit and held it there. Within moments Susie groaned and shifted against him, squirming as if to get away from the intense vibration. Buck kept his other hand against the lips of her pussy and watched, fascinated, as her inner muscles clenched. He could literally feel the wetness seep out of her as he held the massager to her. He lifted it up momentarily and leaned down to kiss her now bright pink clit. "Fucking gorgeous. Again."

Buck had no idea how much time passed, he was lost in the enjoyment of watching Susie orgasm again and again under the vibrations of the Hitachi. He was in control of every single one. She couldn't help but come over and over. Buck alternated between holding the head of the massager against her clit and rubbing hard, and taping her clit steadily and watching her twitch every time he made contact.

The sounds coming out of Susie were reminiscent of the sounds the woman on the video he'd watched made. Low keens, high pitched screams, moans, pleading words and lots of Oh God's and swear words.

"Okay, Sis. You've done so fucking well. I'm so proud of you. One more thing, then I'll let you rest."

"Buck. I can't. I'm so sensitive. I think it actually hurts."

"I know you are, that's why this'll work. I read up on it."

"Oh fuck."

Buck smiled at Susie's words, but turned his attention back to his prize. He held the massager against her breasts for the moment, letting her have a short break from the intense feeling of it against her clit.

He pushed one hand inside her sheath and curled his fingers up until he was touching the front wall of her pussy. He felt her G-spot, and stroked it firmly with one hand. They'd done this before and Susie had always enjoyed it.

"Yeah, Buck. That feels so good. Keep going, right there."

Knowing he'd found the exact spot, he continued to rub against her. Deciding she was ready, he added his middle finger inside. Increasing the rhythm and force of his fingers against her. He could feel her begin to swell a bit, and knew it was time.

Buck got to his knees and shifted so he was next to Susie's hip. He needed more leverage if this was going to work. Susie's eyes were closed and Buck didn't think she even realized he'd moved. He brought the Hitachi down and placed it firmly on her clit as he increased the speed and force of his fingers inside her.

Susie screeched and undulated her hips, trying to simultaneously get away and get closer at the same time. "Buck, Buck, God. Oh my God."

Her words were strained and tight. Buck increased the movements of his fingers inside her even more as he continued to rub the massager hard against her clit. He could tell she had several small orgasms as his hand was covered in her juices, but he wanted that elusive G-spot orgasm, the one that would make her squirt her juices everywhere.

He continued to rub inside her and finally, finally it was done. Buck pulled the massager and his hand away and watched fascinated as her liquid squirted out of her pussy. He dropped the massager on the bed, still running, and put his palm over her clit and rubbed lightly, prolonging her orgasm. She had two or three squirts that continued and she twitched in ecstasy on the bed as she continued to power through the intense G-spot orgasm he'd given her. Her stomach muscles continued to contract and expand and her thighs were straining against their bonds. She moaned continuously at the back of her throat and Buck had never seen anything to beautiful in all his life.

"That's it, Sis, that's it. Fucking beautiful. Look at you. God."

Buck couldn't hold back anymore. He kneeled between her still spasming pussy and shoved himself in to the hilt.

Susie screamed out in pleasure and thrust her hips up to him. "Yeah, yeah, fuck me. Fuck me, Buck."

In all that they'd done, Buck had never felt anything like it before. She was soaked, and he could still feel her juices coming out of her. They covered his balls and her ass as if they were sitting in a hot tub. He thrust in and out, loving how her muscles pulled against him, sucking him in then clenching against him as he pulled out.

"Mine. This pussy is fucking mine," he growled out as he continued to fuck Susie hard. "You hear me, Sis? Mine."

"Yours. Fuck yeah, Buck."

"Milk me. Make me come. I want to fill you so full of my come you'll be dripping it for days."

"Ummmmm, fuck, God. How can I be coming again?" Susie moaned, thrashing her head back and forth. The pillow had long since been knocked out from under her head with her movements and her hair was tangled around her head, sticking to her cheek with sweat. She was covered in a sheen of moisture and Buck thought she'd never looked more beautiful.

"Come with me, Susie. Do it. Come fucking now." Buck thrust inside her as far as he could go and reached over and grabbed the massager. He held the ball to her clit and moaned with her as she immediately started coming again.

"Oh yeah." It was all Buck could get out. The feeling of Susie's muscles squeezing him almost painfully, along with the vibrations from the massager through her walls against his cock, made him lose it. He dropped the massager away and caught himself on his hands as he twitched against her, feeling as if his insides were coming out through his dick.

Finally he collapsed down on his elbows over her, his dick twitching inside her. He could feel Susie's pussy still clenching against him even though he was no longer stimulating her. Without separating himself from her, he reached up and undid the buckles on her wrist cuffs. Susie immediately brought her arms down and clutched his back and drew him down to her. Neither of them said a word, just lay on the bed in the aftermath of the most intense experience either of them had ever had.

Finally, knowing he had to release Susie's ankles and move them to a more comfortable location, Buck reluctantly pulled out of the warm wet cavern he now considered his and groaned as he watched both their juices roll out of her to the sheet underneath. He quickly turned and unbuckled the cuffs around Susie's ankles and turned back to her.

Susie bent her knees and pulled her feet up, but kept her legs open to Buck. He leaned down and licked her folds from bottom to top, enjoying her twitch when he brushed against her clit.

"Buck..."

"I know, Sis, I'm just cleaning you up. Promise." He continued licking up the juices that oozed from her pussy lips and gently eased his finger inside. He stroked and twirled his finger, loving the feel of how wet she was. "Beautiful, simply fucking beautiful."

Finally, knowing Susie was done, as in really done, he scooted over and stood up. He leaned over and picked her up with one hand under her knees and the other under her back. She immediately wrapped her arms around his neck, holding on, not caring where he was going or what he was doing.

He brought her into the bathroom and placed her on her feet, keeping one arm around her while he grabbed a towel. "Hang on the counter for a second." He waited until she was relatively stable and he ran the towel up her legs and over her chest, wiping away her sweat and their juices. He took a corner and cleaned between her legs gently, knowing how sensitive she was there after everything he'd done to her that night.

He briskly ran the towel over himself, making sure most of the wetness was gone from his skin before dropping the towel and picking Susie up again. He walked them down the stairs to the couch. "Grab the blanket." Susie did as he asked and he helped her spread it over the cushions before placing her down on them. "Be right back."

Buck strode back up the stairs, not concerned in the least about his nudity. He came back down carrying their comforter which had been kicked to the ground. He eased down next to Susie and covered them both with the blanket.

"We should clean up."

"I'll do it tomorrow."

"But the bed."

"It's fine, Sis, now shush."

"You should probably stop calling me Sis you know."

"Probably."

"It's kinda gross."

"Do you really care?"

"No."

"Then shush."

"That was..."

Buck kissed Susie on the forehead and pulled her closer. "Yeah."

They fell asleep without another word.

11

LUCKY

Susie came awake slowly the next morning. She shifted, then groaned. Damn she was sore. It all came back to her. Buck. The restraints, the amazing orgasms, the...whatever that was that he'd done there at the end, him fucking her until she almost passed out. Jesus.

She opened her eyes and sat up. She was on the couch, but only vaguely remembered Buck carrying them down the stairs last night. She'd been completely satiated and out of it.

She watched as Buck moved around the kitchen. He was obviously making breakfast.

"Hey." For some reason Susie felt extremely shy after everything that had happened last night. It seemed way more intimate than anything they'd done before...and they'd done a lot before.

Buck was suddenly there. He sat on the couch next to her. He was wearing a pair of jeans which were zipped but not buttoned. He ran his hand over her head and down to her cheek.

"You okay this morning?"

Susie nodded. "Yeah."

"Sore?"

Susie nodded against sheepishly. "Yeah."

"I'd say I was sorry, but I'm not really."

Susie wasn't sure what to say to that, so she didn't say anything.

"Things are different now."

Susie wasn't sure she was ready for this now. "Can I go up and shower before we have this conversation?"

"No." Buck leaned over until Susie didn't have a choice but to fall back. He put his hands on either side of her head on the couch and got close. "I love you."

Wow. He put it right out there. Susie felt her toes curl. He didn't stop there.

"This might have started out weird. We were stepbrother and stepsister, but we aren't anymore. Besides, I wouldn't give a fuck if we were. You're mine. I don't care that you popped my cherry, well, actually I do. You popped it, and you're keeping it."

"Buck…"

"After last night and the way you came apart for me. After the way you trusted me to take care of you? You're mine. I'm not giving it up. I'm not giving you up."

"Don't you want to see what else is out there? I mean, you might regret this."

"Why in the fuck would I want to see what else is out there when I have this?" Buck moved his hand under the blanket, pushing it out of the way as he went, to rest his hand over her folds. He pushed one finger inside her and held her down. "You are absolutely fucking beautiful. You're everything I ever dreamed about when I was jacking myself off. I figured sex would be good, but I had no idea it'd be this good. And that's because of you. I could go out and stick my dick in any ol' hole, but it'd never be like this one." He moved his finger in and out as he spoke, not trying to arouse her, but staking his claim instead.

"We're young, we have our whole lives ahead of us. I'm not proposing, but just the thought of letting you go, eats me up inside. And it's not because of the sex, although that's fucking spectacular. It's you. You're motivated, you can be a bitch, but usually when you think you have a reason to be. You're loyal to your mom and your friends. You want to pull your weight. It's everything."

"Okay, but…"

"And if I have to keep you on your back, tied to my bed, making you squirt all over me, then that's what I'll fucking do. I love you, Susie."

"I love you too." Susie smiled as Buck was silent. Even his finger inside her stilled. She waited for him to work through whatever it was he was working through.

"Fuck yeah you do. Just remember who said it first."

Susie laughed and arched her back. "If I remember, correctly, Bro, I came to you first."

"Oh, you came all right," he retorted.

Susie giggled and leaned up to Buck. She took his face in her hands and kissed him, only moaning a bit when he removed his finger from her folds and pulled back. He stuck his finger in his mouth, never losing eye contact, and licked it clean.

When he was done, he sat up and said, "Go shower, then we'll eat. Then we'll see what else we have to do today. But when we get home, whenever that may be, you'll get naked and take my cock down your throat. It's the least you can do after last night."

Susie thought about giving him a hard time, but

decided he was right. "Okay, I'll grab the sheets and throw them in the wash."

"Already done."

"Really?"

"Yeah."

"Wow."

"Sis, I lived basically on my own for years. You think my Pop did that shit?"

Susie giggled. "I don't know."

Buck held out a hand. "Come on, get upstairs before I decide we're stayin' in today."

Susie stood up with Buck's help and enveloped him in her arms. "Thank you, Buck."

"For what?" His arms immediately wrapped around her back, holding her tightly against him.

"For everything. For saying yes that first night. For not being a dick of a stepbrother. For showing me how good sex can really be. For loving me."

"You don't have to thank me for all that shit."

"Well, thank you anyway."

"You're welcome. Now get your ass upstairs before I do what I threatened earlier. I'll have breakfast waiting for when you come back down."

"Okay." Susie backed away from her former stepbrother and sauntered to the stairs. If she shook her ass a little harder than was strictly necessary to make the short climb, she figured Buck wouldn't complain.

As she showered and changed, Susie had no idea how she'd gotten so lucky. She was a billionaire, but who would've thought her mother's disastrous marriage would've led to her gaining a stepbrother, then a fuck buddy, and now a lover. The world sure worked in weird ways, but she wasn't complaining.

That day, so long ago, when she learned she'd be a stepsister, turned out to be the luckiest day in her life.

~

JOIN my Newsletter and find out about sales, free books, contests and new releases before anyone else!! Click HERE

Want to know when my books go on sale? Follow me on Bookbub HERE!

Would you like Susan's Book Protecting Caroline for FREE?

Click HERE

How about reading Justice for Mackenzie for FREE
as well?
Click HERE

Also by Susan Stoker

Badge of Honor: Texas Heroes Series

Justice for Mackenzie

Justice for Mickie

Justice for Corrie

Justice for Laine (novella)

Shelter for Elizabeth

Justice for Boone

Shelter for Adeline

Shelter for Sophie

Justice for Erin (Nov 2017)

Justice for Milena (Mar 2018)

Shelter for Blythe (July 2018)

Justice for Hope (TBA)

Shelter for Quinn (TBA)

Shelter for Koren (TBA)

Shelter for Penelope (TBA)

Delta Force Heroes Series

Rescuing Rayne

Assisting Aimee - Loosely related to DF

Rescuing Emily

Rescuing Harley

Marrying Emily

Rescuing Kassie

Rescuing Bryn

Rescuing Casey (Jan 2018)

Rescuing Sadie (April 2018)

Rescuing Wendy (May 2018)

Rescuing Mary (Nov 2018)

Ace Security Series

Claiming Grace

Claiming Alexis

Claiming Bailey (Dec 2017)

Claiming Felicity (Mar 2018)

SEAL of Protection: Legacy Series

Defending Caite (TBA)

SEAL of Protection Series

Protecting Caroline

Protecting Alabama

Protecting Fiona

Marrying Caroline (novella)

Protecting Summer

Protecting Cheyenne

Protecting Jessyka

Protecting Julie (novella)

Protecting Melody

Protecting the Future
Protecting Alabama's Kids (novella)
Protecting Kiera (novella)
Protecting Dakota

Stand Alone
The Guardian Mist

Special Operations Fan Fiction
http://www.stokeraces.com/kindle-worlds.html

Beyond Reality Series
Outback Hearts
Flaming Hearts
Frozen Hearts

Writing as Annie George:
Stepbrother Virgin (erotic novella)

ABOUT THE AUTHOR

Annie George is a pen name for a New York Times Best Selling Author. While this is her first erotic venture, she might have some more stories up her sleeve.

Annie lives deep in the heart of Texas and gets her inspiration for her books from the craziness on facebook and her friends.

If you have the time, reviews are always appreciated.

Made in the USA
Columbia, SC
22 December 2024

50433865R00072